George Frederick Maclear

The Slavs

George Frederick Maclear

The Slavs

ISBN/EAN: 9783337403027

Printed in Europe, USA, Canada, Australia, Japan

Cover: Foto ©Andreas Hilbeck / pixelio.de

More available books at **www.hansebooks.com**

CONVERSION OF THE WEST.

THE SLAVS.

BY THE

Rev. G. F. MACLEAR, D.D.,

HEAD MASTER OF KING'S COLLEGE SCHOOL, AUTHOR OF "THE MISSIONS
OF THE MIDDLE AGES," ETC.

WITH MAP.

PUBLISHED UNDER THE DIRECTION OF
THE COMMITTEE OF GENERAL LITERATURE AND EDUCATION,
APPOINTED BY THE SOCIETY FOR PROMOTING
CHRISTIAN KNOWLEDGE.

LONDON:
SOCIETY FOR PROMOTING CHRISTIAN KNOWLEDGE.
SOLD AT THE DEPOSITORIES:
77, GREAT QUEEN STREET, LINCOLN'S-INN FIELDS
4, ROYAL EXCHANGE; 48, PICCADILLY;
AND BY ALL BOOKSELLERS.

NEW YORK: POTT, YOUNG, & CO.
1879.

WYMAN AND SONS, PRINTERS,
GREAT QUEEN STREET, LINCOLN'S INN FIELDS,
LONDON, W.C.

PREFACE.

THE present Volume forms a sequel to and closes the series of those which have been projected on the Conversion of Europe.

In its preparation, as in that of the former Volumes, the most recent and trustworthy authorities have been consulted, and where it has been deemed expedient notes have been subjoined, and references given to larger works.

These it is hoped will increase its value and usefulness.

I cannot, however, allow it to appear without acknowledging the great assistance I have received in its compilation from my sister, Mrs. Herman Gaskoin, who has rendered easy a task which would otherwise have been difficult, if not impossible, amidst my numerous pressing engagements.

G. F. M.

KING'S COLLEGE SCHOOL, LONDON.
March, 1879.

CONTENTS.

CONVERSION OF THE SLAVS.

---◆◇◆---

CHAPTER I.

INTRODUCTION.

IT has been observed that the place of the Slavonic nations in history bears a very small proportion to the space occupied by them on the surface of the globe. They belong to the great Aryan or Indo-European family, and of all its tribes they were almost the last to fall within the focus of historic light. "Their domicile was so remote from the centres of ancient culture, that the Greeks and Romans could scarcely come into direct contact with them ; and having always been, as they are still, by nature a peaceable people, they themselves never greatly interfered in the affairs of their border-lands."[1]

Nevertheless, although until the 6th century these races are unnoticed in the records of Byzantium and of Western Europe, some knowledge of them can be traced back even to the days of Herodotus.

[1] Dr. Vilhelm Thomsen's Lectures on 'The relations between Ancient Russia and Scandinavia,' &c. Lect. i. p. 2. See also Krasinski's 'Lectures on Slavonia.' [Ed. of 1869], p. 1.

The "father of history" himself speaks of the
Callipedæ, the Alazones, and the husbandmen of
Scythia, who have been identified with the Slavo-
nians.

The first Latin author who mentions them is Pliny
the elder, A.D. 79; by him, and by Tacitus, allusion
is made to them under the names of Venedi, Serbi,
and Stavani.   By a form of the first of these names,
"unknown to the Slavonians themselves, the Teutonic
tribes have from the first designated these their eastern
neighbours, viz., *Wends;* and the use of this appellation by the Roman authors plainly shows that their
knowledge of the Slavonians was derived only from the
Germans.   The old German form of this name was
Winedâ, and *Wenden* is the name which the Germans
of the present day give to the remnants of a Slavonic
population, formerly large, who now inhabit Lusatia,
while they give the name of *Winden* to the Slovens
in Carinthia, Carniola, and Styria.   We find the
Anglo-Saxon form, *Winedas, Weonodas,* in King
Alfred's *Orosius,* as a designation of the Wends, or
Slavonians, south of the Baltic; and Vender (in the
Old Norse, *Vindr*) was the name under which this
wild heathen people was known in the North, especially in Denmark, during the middle ages."[1]

"The fifth branch," writes Professor Max Müller,
enumerating the Aryan forms of speech, "which is
commonly called *Slavonic,* I prefer to designate by
the name of *Windic, Winidæ* being one of the most

[1] Dr. Vilhelm Thomsen, Lectures, p. 3.

ancient and comprehensive names by which these tribes were known to the early historians of Europe."[1]

The original native form of the word *Slavonian* was *Slovêne*, but it does not appear that either this, or any other name, was applied by the ancient Slavonians themselves to the whole of their family collectively. On the contrary, "each of the numerous tribes" into which they were divided, "called itself by some peculiar name."[2]

Various derivations have been assigned to the word *Slav*. Some have seen in it a deduction from *Slava*, which, in Slavonic dialects, means *glory*.[3] Nor have reflections been wanting on the singular reversal, in that case, of the bearing of the term. From *glory* its signification has been transformed into *servitude*. In the *Slav*, as reduced to bondage by the Germans, we find the undoubted origin of our word *slave*. "This conversion of a national into an appellative name," says the historian Gibbon, "appears to have arisen in the 8th century, in Oriental France, where the princes and bishops were rich in Slavonian captives."

Others, again, have found the source of this word *Slav*, in *Slovo*, the Slavonic expression for *word*.

---

[1] Lectures on the 'Science of Language,' series i. p. 204.

[2] Dr. Vilhelm Thomsen, p. 4.

[3] "A great number of Slavonic names are unquestionably derived from that word, [*slava*,] as, for instance *Stani-slav*, 'establisher of glory'; *Premi-slav*, 'sense of glory'; *Vladi-slav*, 'ruler of glory,' &c."—Krasinski's Lectures [Ed. 1851], p. 1, note.

These perceive in it an appellation assumed by those who bore it, in proud contradistinction from alien races. For the Slavonians habitually applied to the Germans, and other foreigners, the term *Niem*, or *mute*, thereby implying that they admitted no language but their own to be articulate, and regarded themselves as the only people gifted with true *words*, or speech.[1]

When the Roman Empire was crumbling into decay, cohesion giving place to disunion, and strength dwindling into impotence, the scene of her declining majesty was overrun and occupied by hordes of barbarous strangers. Briefly and broadly classifying them, these peoples fall easily into three groups,— the *Celts*, the *Teutons*, and the *Slavs*.

In this triple distribution the Slavonic nations take third rank, because, although the Teutonic immigration occurred at a somewhat later date than their own, they were soon outstripped in point of culture, both social and moral, by the Teutons, who also anticipated them in their relations with the moribund Empire.

The most ancient home of the Slavonians, of which we have any knowledge, lay in a region whose boundaries may thus be defined :—on the west, the river Vistula; on the east, the river Dnieper, or the district immediately beyond it; on the south, the Carpathian mountains. On the north, it is thought,

---

[1] Krasinski's Lectures [Ed. 1851], note, p. 2. Stanley's 'Eastern Church,' p. 285.

it may have stretched beyond the Dwina, towards what was afterwards called Novgorod.[1]

The cause of the Slavonian descent on the imperial frontiers can only be conjectured. The movement is supposed to have been, in the first instance, compulsory, and due to pressure in the rear from nations dwelling beyond the north-eastern border of the Slavs. This view is confirmed by an examination of the nature of the immigration, as well as of the characteristics of the immigrants.

Unlike the Teutonic tribes, the Slavs did not press forward at once in the direction of the heart of the Empire. They must have halted not very far within the Roman boundaries. For it was only gradually that they became known to the inhabitants of Western Europe, and not until after the Teutonic races had conquered and settled in the south-western imperial provinces. For some time, indeed, they contented themselves with treading in the first footsteps of the Teutonic invaders. They quietly took possession of lands abandoned, after temporary occupation, by the Teutons, who had pushed impatiently onward, bent on exploring the interior of the Roman dominions.

It is also to be remarked, that the Slavonic tribes were by no means distinguished either for a love of arms or adventure, or for any capacity for warfare. They were found, indeed, at a very early period, among the Goths on the banks of the Don, and sub-

---

[1] Dr. Vilhelm Thomsen, p. 4.

sequently with the Huns and Bulgarians on the Danube ; and they took part in several of the memorable incursions of those fierce races, which agitated the Roman Empire so profoundly. But it was generally in the character of hired auxiliaries, allies, or, more often still, vassals, that they were incorporated with the armies of other nations. In their wild homes beyond the Carpathians they led a peaceful and monotonous life. Little molested, probably, among those unattractive wastes of forest and marsh land, they were never either aggressive or ambitious, and played no part in the events occurring beyond their own borders.

From this brief consideration of the antecedents of the Slavs, we pass to a survey of their characteristics, at the time when they had freshly exchanged their original haunts for settlements within the confines of the Empire.

Theirs was no savage rush upon defenceless lands, no frightful pathway of blood and fire cleft through a shuddering civilization. They were not the scourge and terror of Europe, as the Celts had been, nor were they haunted, like their Teutonic neighbours, by a spirit of incessant restlessness, nor consumed by a thirst for plunder and conquest. They neither menaced the Empire nor assaulted its outposts. Their natural tendencies, on the contrary, were of a tranquil kind. The life they had led among the remote Scythian marshes was reproduced in their new quarters, and their aim, as immigrants, seems to have been simply to turn their present more favourable conditions to account, in the expansion of the habits which had hitherto, by force of circumstances, been only imperfectly developed.

We have seen that the Slavs began by quietly occupying lands evacuated by the Teutons. These they diligently cultivated. They grew and stored large quantities of corn. They owned valuable and increasing herds of cattle. They were brewers of mead, fruit-growers, shepherds,—proficients in the agriculture of the age.

Nor did they, as time wore on, confine themselves to a pastoral life. Their peaceful habits of industry naturally developed a taste and an aptitude for commerce. They sought, and found, a market for the products of their labour.

On the shores of the Baltic, Slavonian towns were gradually built, of which Lubeck was the first. Among these primitive seaports, one, situated at the mouth of the Oder, and known as Vineta, or Julin, has been called the 'Slavonic Amsterdam.' Trading connections were opened between the Baltic and the Black seas. Kief was built on the banks of the Dnieper, and Novgorod on the Wolkhow. Both these towns rapidly rose into commercial importance. In Germany mines were sunk. Metals were smelted and cast. Salt became an article of export.

It is clear that the Slavonic population, devoted to the profitable pursuits just indicated, must have been highly beneficial to the countries they inhabited. What those countries were it is time that we should turn back to inquire.

In a map illustrating the early part of the 6th century we find the Slavs represented as consisting of three principal divisions, each embracing a number of subordinate tribes. On the east lay the *Antes*. They extended from the Dniester eastward to the Dnieper and the Don, and southward as far as the shores of the Euxine. The western branch, called the *Venedi*, or *Wends*, inhabited the shores and neighbourhood of the Baltic. The central body, known as the *Slavenes*, was a nomad race. These intermingled, from time to time, with both the eastern and western wings of the great settlement.[1]

As time went by, the Slavonians gradually and steadily extended their borders, spreading eastward, southward, and westward. North of the Carpathians, their territories included the areas of Pomerania, Mecklenburg, Brandenburg, Saxony, Lusatia, Bohemia, Moravia, and Silesia, as well as Poland and Russia. South of the same mountains, they occupied Moldavia and Wallachia, and they established the kingdoms of Slavonia, Bosnia, Servia, and Dalmatia; they were found in Pannonia, and they penetrated as far as Illyria and Carinthia.[2]

The occupiers of this vast tract of country were, at the outset, most simple and rude in their manner of

---

[1] "The best modern writers on the history and languages of the Slavonians have divided the nation into two great branches, a western one corresponding to the Sclaveni, and an eastern one corresponding to the Antes, the distinction between these being founded upon the languages spoken by the tribes belonging to either division."—Smith's Gibbon [Ed. 1854], p. 168, note.

[2] See Krasinski's Lectures [Ed. 1851], p. 3.

life. They were satisfied to live in miserable huts of roughly hewn timber, to fare frugally and coarsely, and to confine their wants to the fewest possible. Most of the early writers, however, have something favourable to say of them. Procopius asserts that they were artless and kind, as well as generous. Adam of Bremen testifies to their lavish hospitality. It was recorded by the emperor Maurice[1] that their prisoners were not doomed to perpetual bondage, but, if not ransomed by their countrymen, were liberated after a given time, and allowed to live among their captors on a free and friendly footing. The biographer of bishop Otho of Bamberg bears witness to the honesty of the race, remarking that the Pomeranians never found it necessary to keep anything under lock and key. "They were much astonished," he writes, "when they beheld the chests and trunks of the bishop locked." The same author relates the significant circumstance, that these Slavonians of Pomerania grounded their chief objection to Christianity on the dishonesty and immorality of its professors.[2] But this is to anticipate.

Free alike from care and from ambition, these early Slavonians were a cheerful, light-hearted race, keenly alive to enjoyment, and entering with zest into such homely pleasures as their circumscribed interests afforded them. Though not without latent courage, and readiness to defend themselves when attacked, they displayed none of that ferocious

---

[1] 'Stratagems,' lib. xi. cap. viii.
[2] Krasinski's Lectures [Ed. 1869], p. 25.

vehemence which we are accustomed to associate with the races who ran riot over the mouldering Empire. "Their courage," says Mr. Sheppard, "is more passive than active in its character, and the Slavonian blood is deficient in that fiery ardour, the *élan* which precipitates the Frank and his kindred races upon the foe." [1]

Into war, when war thrust itself upon them, the Slavs rushed almost without clothing, protecting themselves with the shield alone, and fitting poisoned arrows to their bows. They were skilled in the use of the lasso, and as spearmen were not to be despised, particularly in single combat. "In the field the Slavonian infantry was dangerous, by their speed, agility, and hardiness; they swam, they dived, they remained under water, drawing their breath through a hollow cane; and a river, or lake, was often the scene of their unsuspected ambuscade. But these were the achievements of spies or stragglers; the military art was unknown to them." [2]

From the slight sketch already presented of the manners and customs of the ancient Slavonians, we easily infer that they must have offered a peculiarly tempting prey to races of a different calibre. They became the victims of a long course of tyranny and oppression.

As early as the 3rd or 4th century, before their pristine settlements were broken up, they bent

---

[1] 'The Fall of Rome, and Rise of the Nationalities,' p. 146.
[2] Gibbon, vol. v. p. 229.

their necks under the Gothic yoke. The Goths, under their leader Ermanarik, conquered the western part of the country now called Russia. But they did not long linger so far north, and the Slavs were relieved of their masters after a short submission.[1] Bondage of a darker type, however, awaited them. It has been hinted that they were from time to time forced into war on behalf of their barbarian neighbours, and compelled to fight for the interests of those who were fiercer than themselves. Let us take a single instance of this species of early thraldom. Conquered, towards the end of the 6th century, by the terrible Avars, many Slavic tribes passed through a scathing ordeal, thus graphically described by an author already quoted. " In peace their houses, their flocks, and herds, and fields, their wives and daughters, were at the disposal of their brutal masters, while they were themselves driven away into the depths of forests and morasses, yet all the while compelled to keep up the payment of a burdensome tribute. In war their position was more terrible still. Driven to the field in herds, before the Avar warriors, they were placed, though imperfectly armed, in the front of the battle, and compelled to meet the shock of the imperial legionary, with his iron-clad body and sweeping sword. If they recoiled, as they necessarily must, they were goaded onward by the pike of their masters and allies in the rear."[2] Thus

---

[1] Dr. Vilhelm Thomsen, p. 5.

[2] Sheppard's ' Rise of the Nationalities,' p. 217. Hence the Slavs acquired the epithet of "*Bifurci*," or "pricked on both sides."

were these unfortunate people,—deficient as they were in martial instinct,—of whom Gibbon writes that "their name was obscure, and their conquests inglorious,"[1] compelled to bear the brunt of savage wars in which they had not a particle of interest. Defenceless, despised, and held of no more account than dumb beasts, they awaken in us necessarily—though we perceive them but dimly across the centuries—feelings of the deepest compassion.

At this stage of their existence, however, the Slavs had not, as we have seen, anything of their own to forfeit, beyond the right of every human being to live. At a later period, when they were not only independent, but raised by their own exertions to a position of commercial prosperity unusual for their day, they fared worse, because they lost more, than before.

Systematically crushed, degraded, and oppressed by the Germans on the one hand, by the Turks on the other, and, finally, by the Mongols to the eastward, it was not wonderful that the typical virtues of the Slavs, rude as they were, gradually declined and finally disappeared, to make room for qualities and capabilities of an infinitely lower character.

Mingled motives probably inspired the onslaught of their enemies. Of these, it is natural to suppose that cupidity was the most powerful. The religious element may not indeed be wholly excluded. For here, as everywhere in those dark ages, the light vouchsafed to guide men's lives burned but dimly, and the Cross was often thrust forward as the initial

[1] Vol. v. p. 230.

symbol of lamentable cruelty. Besides, as we shall presently see, the Slavonians were wedded to their idols with a persistent tenacity peculiarly calculated to provoke the rough reformers of the period. But it cannot be doubted that commercial advantages so patent as theirs must have constituted a very strong temptation to more powerful and less prosperous races. Fortitude under protracted suffering, and unusual powers of passive endurance, have been claimed as attributes of the Slavs by an able apologist of their cause. He institutes a comparison in this respect, between them and the North American Indians, whose resolute demeanour under torture is well known.[1] These qualities were destined to be severely tried.

The sufferings of this people seem to have culminated in Germany. There, persecution may be said to have befallen them both collectively and individually.

On the one hand, whole provinces were reduced to slavery, while entire populations were not only banished from the towns which were occupied by German colonists, but were crippled by sweeping commercial disabilities, and impoverished by the compulsory payment of heavy tribute.

On the other hand, the life of the individual could not be called his own. Although his wife and family may not have been the absolute property of his masters, as under the Avar *régime*, his liberty was curtailed to such an extent that its very name became a mockery. He was an exile from every community

---

[1] Krasinski [1869], p. 30.

except that one in which he was peremptorily ordered
to dwell.   If he ventured beyond a certain distance
from this appointed place, and could produce no
satisfactory reason for the irregularity, he was liable
to instant death.   At Hamburg, an enactment provided that every person desirous of becoming a
burgher must furnish proof that he was not even of
Slavonic descent.

When the bishop of Oldenburg visited Lubeck, for
the purpose of admonishing the Slavs of the Baltic
for their idolatry and other malpractices, and of urging
them to exchange their corrupt faith for the purer
creed of Christianity, he was thus addressed by one
of the Slavonic chiefs :—" Oh ! venerable prelate !
your words are the words of God, and useful for our
salvation ; but how can we follow the way which you
are pointing out to us, when we are entangled in so
many evils ?   Our princes oppress us with such severity, and impose upon us such tributes and servitude,
that *death is become more desirable to us than life.* This
very year, we, the inhabitants of this little corner,
have paid to the duke 1,000 marks, and 100 to the
count, and yet this is not sufficient, and we are
squeezed unto exhaustion every day.   How shall we
then attend to this new religion ?   If we cross the
Travena—in Holstein—the same calamities await us ;
if we retire to the river Panis—in Pomerania—it is
still the same.   What, then, remains to us except to
leave the earth, to go to the sea, and to live upon the
waves ?   Is it, then, our fault if, expelled from our
country, we disturb the sea, and levy on the Danes,

or on the merchants who navigate it, our means of living? Are not our princes answerable for this mischief to which they compel us?" There is a touch of pathos in the respectful name, *our princes*, thus applied to the ruthless conquerors whose iron yoke galled the speaker's countrymen almost into madness. "The wild but plaintive spirit of the hereditary bondman," says Mr. Sheppard, "yet lives in his national music, as it breaks upon the ear in the low, melancholy wail of the wind instruments from the bands of Croat and Slavonian regiments, on the Glacis of Vienna."[1]

Oppression had its way. Cruelty begat cruelty. The wind having been diligently sown, the whirlwind was duly reaped. The Slavonic character was slowly metamorphosed. Gentleness degenerated into an apathetic indolence, frankness gave place to cunning, manliness was lost in servility. The time came when the long oppressed gloried in oppressing. They who had writhed in the dust at the feet of contemptuous tyrants exulted at last, in setting an iron heel on the necks of those whom they found to be weaker than themselves.

On this melancholy passage from honour to dishonour it is not needful to dwell further. The story of this group of nationalities after their contact with the Empire, has been sufficiently unrolled to show how the cithern[2] came to be replaced by the dagger,

[1] 'Nationalities,' p. 146.
[2] Byzantine writers report that the Slavonians were a very musical people. "The cithern is mentioned as a favourite instrument among them."

and pastoral hospitalities by deadly and suspicious hatred.

Before drawing these introductory observations to a close, it remains to invite attention to the geographical features of the regions peopled by the Slavonic races.

For it were a mistake to suppose that the surroundings of nature are effectless upon the character of any people. They reflect themselves upon humanity in varying degrees of vividness.

The mountain has a mysterious power over those who creep about its foot; the forest uplifts, with its mighty branches, the thoughts of the humblest wanderer in its shade; the sea has a voice, unheard by the multitude, for those who commune with it in all its changing moods.

But the connection between the features of the landscape and the moral and mental development of the men who daily behold them, is perhaps more intimate, as it certainly is more visible, in the primitive condition of a society, than at a later stage of its growth.[1] It follows, that where such growth has been slow and inconsiderable, the connection in question continues to be clearly apparent, even after the lapse of many generations.

The very word *Oriental* conjures up a vision of still life. In the East, the region of speculative immobility, are no rapid changes, no violent reactions, no sudden innovations. There, the Present faithfully

---

[1] Stanley's 'Eastern Church,' p. 292.

illustrates the Past, because it is a reiteration of it. "The Eastern Church," says a well-known writer, "was like the East, stationary and immutable ; the Western, like the West, progressive and flexible. This distinction is the more remarkable, because at certain periods of their course, there can be no doubt that the civilization of the Eastern Church was far higher than that of the Western." Again : " the East holds the chief place in the monastic world. The words which describe the state are not Latin, but Greek or Syriac,—*Hermit, monk, anchoret, monastery, cœnobite, ascetic, abbot, abbey.* And not only was monasticism born in the Eastern Church; it has also thriven there with unrivalled intensity. Indeed, the earliest source of monastic life is removed even further than the Thebaid deserts, in the Manichean repugnance of the distant East towards the material world, as it is exhibited under its simplest form in the Indian Yogi, or the Mussulman Fakir. It is this Oriental seclusion which, whether from character, or climate, or contagion, has to the Christian world been far more forcibly represented in the Oriental than in the Latin Church. Active life is, on the strict Eastern theory, an abuse of the system." [1]

The relevancy of the foregoing reflections to our immediate subject is easily demonstrable. In the story of " the Conversion of the Slavs," the Byzantine Church figures prominently. So closely and continuously is its instrumentality interwoven with

[1] ' Eastern Church,' p. 26.

the work of enlightenment,[1] that no preliminary survey of the field to be traversed in this treatise would be complete without a briefly comprehensive glance at its position, its character, and its machinery. All these, according to the author above quoted, were subtilely blended with the natural bias arising from the geographical configuration of the lands over which Oriental influence brooded. Before pursuing in his own words this interesting line of thought, let us ourselves look round over the countries of Slavonic adoption. For a large proportion of them are identical with the domains of the Eastern Church.

We are at once impressed with the vastness, the vagueness, the dreaminess, on every side.

The eye travels over broad, level expanses, loses itself in shadowy distances, and is confused by indefinite boundary-lines.

The idea of space transcends every other.

The element of the picturesque may indeed seem wanting. It could hardly translate itself into conditions so large. Where the horizon is so distant and so wide, the foreground does not challenge concentrated attention.

But while our gaze wanders across the great, green plains, through which stately rivers roll slowly towards invisible seas, we become conscious of that "lulling effect of almighty sight and sound, which all feel and none define (it would be less sacred if more

---

[1] "The conversion of the Slavonic races was to the Church of Constantinople, what the conversion of the Teutonic races was to the Church of Rome."—Stanley's 'Eastern Church,' p. 287.

explicable)," and are aware that we behold "repose, expressed in matter."[1]

"Look for a moment," exclaims the writer from whose musings we have been digressing :—"look for a moment at the countries included within the range of the Oriental churches. What they lose in historical, they gain in geographical grandeur. Their barbarism and their degradation have bound them to local peculiarities, from which the more progressive Church of the West has shaken itself free. It is a Church, in fact, not of cities and villages, but of mountains, and rivers, and caves, and dens of the earth. The eye passes from height to height, and rests on the successive sanctuaries in which the religion of the East has intrenched itself, as within huge, natural fortresses, against its oppressors :—Athos, in Turkey ; Sinai, in Arabia ; Mar Saba, in Palestine ; Ararat, in Armenia ; the cedars of Lebanon ; the catacombs of Kieff ; ·the cavern of Megaspelion ; the cliffs of Meteora. Or we see it, advancing up and down the streams, or clinging to the banks of the mighty rivers which form the highways and the arteries of the wide plains of the East. The Nile still holds its sacred place in the liturgies of Egypt. The Jordan, from Constantine downwards, has been the goal of every Eastern pilgrim. Up the broad stream of the Dnieper sail the first apostles of Russia. Along the Volga and the Don cluster the mysterious settlements of Russian nonconformity."[2]

---

[1] Ruskin's 'Modern Painters,' vol. ii. p. 64.
[2] 'Eastern Church,' pp. 3, 4.

Reference has been made to the immovable dogged-
ness with which the Slavonic races were found to
cling to their early pagan creed.   Before opening the
story of the torchbearers who braved the gloom
whence these tribes were so reluctant to emerge,
it would therefore seem that some attention should
be bestowed on the shadowy, idol-peopled sphere of
Slavic heathenism itself.

For it is natural to inquire into the character of
the influences which were found so powerful by all
who sought to undermine them.   A constitutional
slowness in mental movement, even when enhanced
by a strong aversion to change as change, cannot be
held entirely accountable for tenacity[1] such as the
Slavs will be found displaying in their hold upon
their ancient superstitions.

---

[1] Apropos of this peculiar tenacity, the subjoined reference,
by the author of "The Foregleams of Christianity" [Charles
Newton Scott], to Count de Gobineau's 'valuable remarks on
the inflexible adherence of the Asiatics even to forms of worship
dating from a remote antiquity,' will not be without interest :
"Tous ces chœurs que je viens de décrire ; confréries dansant
sur place, berbérys, corps de ballet, tout cela est l'héritage de
la plus haute antiquité.   Rien n'y est changé, ni la musique des
tambourins, ni les battements de poitrine, ni les cantiques, ni les
litanies.   Les noms des divinités sont autres, voilà tout, et la
Perse moderne entoure ses tazyèhs des mêmes cérémonies, des
mêmes expiations, de la même pompe qui se voyaient jadis aux
fêtes d'Adonis.   Ce n'est pas un médiocre sujet de réflexion que
de voir partout et toujours cette Asie si tenace dans ses résolu-
tions, dans ses admirations, braver et traverser deux cultes aussi
puissants que le Christianisme et l'Islam, pour conserver ou
reprendre ses plus anciennes habitudes."   P. 32, note.

CHAPTER II.

SLAVONIC HEATHENDOM.

THE simplicity which marked the mode of life of the ancient Slavs reflected itself in their religious system. This was less elaborate than that either of the Teutons or Scandinavians. " As their supreme god," we are briefly told by one historian, " the Slavonians adored an invisible master of the thunder. The rivers and the nymphs obtained their subordinate honours, and the popular worship was expressed in vows and sacrifice." [1]

The earliest attainable information on this subject is to be gathered from Procopius. He tells us that the Slavonic people were no believers in fate, and that they originally worshipped the Thundermaker as the sole lord of the universe, to whom sacrifices of various kinds were imperatively due. This being was impersonated at Novgorod, Kief, and elsewhere, by an idol known as Perun,[2] which was constructed of wood, with a head of silver adorned by golden whiskers. Of the great respect entertained for this image we shall find abundant proof in future pages.

Some temples, again, contained idols of fantastic

[1] Gibbon, v. p. 229.

[2] Perun may be taken as answering to the *Paranjya* of the Vedas. The Slavonic Dazhbog, the day-god, and Stribog, the wind-god, have also their counterparts in the old Aryan nature-worship.

shapes, conceived in the fertile imaginations of their
devotees. Of this kind was a celebrated image at
Plumen, or Plön, in Holstein. As among the Teutonic races, indeed, the primitive idea of a single,
supreme god, which Perun represented, seems to have
been gradually modified into an admission of various
subordinate claims to divinity. The woods were held
to be the haunts of certain deities, who were however
unrepresented by any figures, and unassociated with
any fixed shrines. We read that "the belief in fairies
and other imaginary beings, inhabiting the woods, the
water, and the air, still lingers among the peasantry of
many Slavonic countries, and is preserved in a great
number of popular tales, songs, and superstitious
observances."[1] When death seemed imminent, from
illness or by the sword, it was the custom of the
Slavonians to register solemn vows that, in the event
of recovery or deliverance, they would offer sacrifices
of thanksgiving to their gods. And, the threatened
danger once past, they were invariably careful to
fulfil all such engagements.

A characteristic feature of their religion was a par-
tiality for many-headed divinities. Of this grotesque
kind was Triglav,—whose triple head, we shall find,
was preserved when his body was destroyed at Stettin,
as a curiosity worth sending to the pope,—and,
again, Radegast, the god of war. When Danish
missionaries forced their way at last into the island of
Rügen, they found that fastness of Slavonic heathenism

---

[1] Krasinski [1869], p. 15.

teeming with monstrous figures of this description. At Arcona, the capital, among other temples, stood that of the great Svantovit, the favourite idol of the Baltic Slavonians. The circumstances under which this image was destroyed will be detailed in their proper place. But a sketch of the figure itself could scarcely be excluded with propriety from this preliminary endeavour to picture to ourselves the Slavonic conceptions of supernatural majesty and power.

We are indebted for the description of Svantovit to a Danish historian, who may not improbably have been an eye-witness of his demolition. The temple which enclosed the god was in itself a model of beauty and symmetry. It was built of wood, and consisted of an outer and an inner court. The roof of the outer enclosure was painted red, and the inner division of the building was decorated with paintings, and draped with tapestry. Here stood Svantovit, whose enormous size and plurality of members may well have amazed an unaccustomed spectator. He possessed four heads, four necks, two chests, and two backs, and in his great right hand he grasped a horn, variously composed of blended metals, which was once a year filled by the priest in attendance, with mead. His left arm was bent in the shape of a bow, while his lower limbs were concealed by long drapery, which fell to his feet. His sword, enriched with a silver hilt and scabbard, lay, with his bridle, beside him.[1]

The worship of so magnificent a deity was neces-

[1] In the Teutonic religious system, the Saxon Irmin-Saule was, in many particulars, the corresponding deity to Svantovit.

sarily expensive, and its cost was met in several ways. Besides an annual tax paid by the inhabitants of the island, a third of the booty seized in war was devoted to this object, irrespectively of the many offerings which were presented at the temple by opulent chiefs. A picked cavalry detachment, numbering three hundred men, was devoted to the special service of Svantovit. These troopers fought in the god's name, and all the spoil wrested by them from the enemy was considered his peculiar property and used by the priest, so far as it was available for ornamenting his temple.] Svantovit also possessed a horse, on which his presence was believed invisibly to accompany the army in time of war. This animal was spotlessly white, and was regarded with such awe, that a priest only was allowed either to feed or to mount him, and it was accounted a sin to draw a single hair out of his mane or his tail. The sacred horse of Svantovit was further solemnly consulted as an oracle, when war was about to be declared. Three rows of spears having been laid on the ground in front of the temple, special prayers were addressed to its august inmate, after which the horse was led out by the attendant priest. The movements of his feet were watched with great anxiety, for if, in stepping over the spears, he lifted his right hoof first, the omen was favourable, and the proposed expedition might safely be undertaken. If, on the other hand, the left foot was first raised, or both feet moved together, it was a sign that it must be promptly abandoned. ⌐ ˙

But the greatest solemnity conducted under the auspices of Svantovit, occurred after the ingathering of harvest. The inhabitants assembled from all parts of Rügen, and celebrated a feast, which was duly inaugurated by liberal sacrifices of cattle. The priest, venerable and solemn, with hair unshorn, and beard unclipped, first entered the inner enclosure of the temple, and swept it with reverent care. During this process he was obliged to guard against defiling the presence of the god by holding his breath, and if respiration became, as it must repeatedly have become, necessary, he withdrew to indulge in it in the outer air. When all was ready, he took the mead-cup, before mentioned, from the hand of Svantovit, and bore it forth to the multitude outside. From the state of its contents he augured the fortune to be expected in the coming year. If the mead had decreased in quantity since its solemn inpouring at the last festival, scarcity was impending. But if it had increased, the people might confidently reckon on abundance. In either case, the year-old mead was emptied at the feet of the god as a libation, and the priest proceeded to re-fill the horn, praying at the same time for prosperity and for success in war. His next step was to drink the freshly dedicated mead at a draught, and he then once more poured the prescribed amount into the horn, which was replaced in the idol's hand, there to be undisturbed until the next annual festival. Sweet circular cakes of honey and flour were afterwards offered, and the ceremonial observances ended in a general benediction on the part of the priest, who in this act personated the god, and accompanied his blessing with exhortations to continual sacrifices, which, he assured the people, would find their reward in the victory over all enemies so ardently coveted. Feasting followed, and the revellers were encouraged, if not commanded, to give an unbridled rein to their appetites.[1]

In Rügen, as will later be recorded, other gods of a stamp not dissimilar to Svantovit were found in abundance. There was the image of Porenut, the deity presiding over the seasons, with five faces, the fifth being on his breast. There also towered Rhugevit, with his seven faces and his eight swords.[2]

But enough has been said to show the character of the Slavonic ritual up to a date as late, even, as the year A.D. 1168. We must now consider with care the principles on which it was based.

As in other pre-Christian systems of religion, we find among the Slavonians—and, perhaps, to a somewhat unusual degree—that bewildered recognition of the unfathomable mysteries thronging the road of human life, which is co-existent even with the present broad flood of Gospel light.

The solemn silence of the unseen world,—the beauty and the grandeur of the visible universe, with the pain, the sorrow, the sin, that shadow it,— the contradictory impulses of the human heart, the

---

[1] Saxo Grammaticus. *Historiæ Danicæ*, lib. xiv.

[2] The Lettic tribes added a god in the form of a bird to their catalogue of divinities.

ever-brooding presence of gigantic power held in leash, the strange dissonances of life which none knew how to resolve into concord,—these enigmas confronted the ancients as they confront us now, but without the key by which it is permitted to us, in some degree, to solve them. In our day, the possessors of "the tranquillity of deep and living faith, are most conscious that in the kingdoms both of grace and nature, in the volume of God's works, and in the volume of His Word, a thousand difficulties remain, which they are utterly unable to decipher; depths of thought they never hope to fathom, discords which they cannot harmonize, and elevations which they cannot climb."

"A man of this kind"—it has, again, been well said —"knows in what he has believed; and though he still sees darkly, communing with adumbrations of the truth, and not with truth itself, he waits in patience till that veil which separates the present from the future has been finally withdrawn, till Christianity has been divested of the earthly symbols under which it is presented to his faith, and he beholds it as it is. What happens in the physical world as the reward of patient observation, will, he is persuaded, happen also in the moral world. The seeming incongruities will form at last a *concordissima dissonantia*, and the riddles that now test and try us will be then converted into proofs of harmony and vehicles of love."[1]

To many among ourselves, the 'silence of God' is

---

[1] Hardwick's 'Christ and other Masters,' pp. 8, 9.

profoundly impressive. He *has* spoken, indeed, and by His Blessed Revelation we hold fast. But it seems to us long ago ; and since those Divine utterances died away, there has been no sign, no voice nor language from heaven to earth, of such a kind that all must needs hear and heed. The thought presents itself to us again and again,—but it does not agitate us, because of the Holy Whisperings which the heart of each man can detect in its own depths, —because of the never-ceasing call of Providence in circumstances, which none who watch them can deny,—and because the written Word we grasp, containing all things necessary to our salvation, requires no codicil. But when the early Slavonians, and their unenlightened contemporaries, stood, with bated breath, face to face with the gaugeless problems of life and death, the unbroken silence beyond the gates of the Invisible must have seemed oppressive indeed. For, as far as their knowledge went, the Divine Voice had not spoken at all, and they were fain to grope, in gross darkness, for such a clue as they could find or fashion.

We have already noted that the Slavonians were conspicuous as sufferers at the hands of other peoples. They were only too familiar, from very early times, with the dark side of life, and it was natural that they should transport the colouring of their practical experience into the character of the religion which they systematized. We accordingly find *fear* to be the predominant element in it.

Everywhere, in the worlds of nature and of humanity, they beheld an unceasing strife, marked by violent fluctuations and constant vicissitudes, between two warring powers. They accounted for this double agency of good and evil, by the supposition that a duality of gods exercised an ever-conflicting sway over the fortunes of mortals, and they met, or hoped to meet it, by every conceivable device to magnify the good, while they propitiated the evil, divinities.[1]

Like the Mexicans and the South Sea Islanders, they ascribed every event in life to the influence either of the "white," *i.e.* the benignant, or of the "black," *i.e.* the malevolent, invisible powers.

Though a devout worshipper of the beneficent "sun-god," and other good and generous agents, "the rude American," writes Mr. Hardwick, "was haunted by the thought of some co-equal and co-ordinate array of hostile deities, who manifested their malignant nature by creating discord, sickness, death, and every possible form of evil. Everywhere the worship of the Indian was mainly occupied in deprecating powerful and malevolent spirits, demons, spectres, fiends, hobgoblins, whose errand was to poison human joys and aggravate the load of human wretchedness. If only the American could turn away

---

[1] "Dualism is not merely the perception of a difference between right and wrong, for, since man has been man, his moral sense must have been more or less in activity, but it is the perception of a *radical* difference, of a difference at least sufficiently accentuated to be the basis of the classification which men consciously or unconsciously make of things external to themselves."—'Foregleams of Christianity,' p. 51.

their anger, and evade or disappoint their malice, he
had realized the principal aim of his religion.   Hence
his constant dread of some unearthly apparition.
Hence the meaning of his fetishes, his amulets, his
charms, his exorcisms, his trembling and convulsive
efforts to explore the secrets of the past or future, his
wild cries and frantic dances.   Hence, again, the
vast ascendancy obtained by seers and witches,
payés, jossakeeds, and medicine-men, with other dark
and nameless instruments of heathen sorcery." [1]

Again.   " The dread of malevolent beings [in
Oceanica] far outbalances the hope inspired among
these tribes by vague ideas respecting the beneficence
of other spirits ; and as happiness itself is seldom
there associated with the presence of moral qualities,
either in the judge or in the human subject, but is
treated merely as the fruit of chance or of caprice,
the sentiment of fear is still more terribly awakened
whensoever the Vitian,[2] in the hours of silence or of
sickness, listens to the beating of his inmost heart,
and communes more directly with the world invisible." [3]

Once more.   " The gloomy terror everywhere inspired alike by the religions of the wild American and
by those of Oceanica, has found its counterpart again
among the various tribes of Central Africa."   " Their
religion, if such it may be called, is one of dread.

---

[1] 'Christ and other Masters,' pp. 358, 359.
[2] Allusion is here being made specially to the inhabitants of
the Fiji—or *Viti*—and neighbouring islands.
[3] Ibid., p. 397.

Numbers of charms are employed to avert the evils with which they feel themselves to be encompassed. There is nothing more heartrending than their death wails."[1]

This triple illustration of the bondage of fear, thus represented as enthralling these widely severed groups of heathen, is here adduced, because it depicts with equal accuracy the mainspring of the ancient Slavonic religious system.[2]

Cringing fear begets unscrupulous barbarity, and the worship of Zernabog, the chief among the "black"—or sinister—powers adored by the Slavonians, was disfigured by human sacrifices, and polluted by rites, from the details of which their very chronicler might be pardoned for recoiling in horror. For apart from "the instinct of expiation," which the Slavonic people shared, more or less consciously, with all other divisions of the human family, it was naturally concluded that the powers of death and darkness could find no satisfaction in observances or in offerings which did not partake of their own fierce and sanguinary nature.

---

[1] Ibid., p. 582. And Dr. Livingstone, as there quoted.

[2] The native Indians of *South* America, also, are dominated by terror. With reference to them, Dr. J. G. Müller says : " Man sieht, dass auch hier das Schauerliche und Furchter-regende vorherrscht ; Furcht ist ja das Grundgefühl, das durch das Vernehmen des Göttlichen auch bei diesen Naturmenschen erregt wird ; die ganze Natur ist von einer Unzahl von Geistern erfüllt, die bei Tag und bei Nacht, beim Schlafen und beim Wachen, Welt und Seele mit Angst und Schauder erfüllen." —P. 83, quoted in ' Christ and other Masters,' p. 360, note.

We turn away with a feeling of relief to glance, though it can be only momentarily, at the more peaceful side of the picture.

Lada was the Slavonic goddess of love and pleasure.

Kupala was the god of the fruits of the earth.

And Koleda, the god of festivals. In various parts of Russia and Poland, the name of *Koleda* is even now given to the feast of Christmas.

In festive honour of *St. John Kupala*, youths still dance round lighted fires in some Slavonian countries, on the 23rd of June, the eve of St. John the Baptist's day.

An outline has now been drawn of the wild Slavonic cult, to the practices of which its believers were attached with a persistency which we shall find repeating itself, as we pass from country to country, with redoubled, and again redoubled, emphasis. It is only an outline; and here and there,—as, for example, in Prussia,—the local usages and beliefs, when stamped with unusual clearness upon a particular people or district, will help, as we go on, to fill it in.

But before concluding this introductory sketch of the Slavonic mythology, it may be observed that no Celtic community ever paid more profound respect to the Druids, in whom its members loved to recognize their guardians and their presidents, than that accorded by the Slavs to their priests.

The priesthood blended and monopolized functions both civil and religious. Its power was never questioned, and in some cases deference as servile as it was extravagant was exacted from the people.

This implicit submissiveness will scarcely surprise us after a moment's reflection on the service of abject terror, which we have seen that the dualistic religion of the Slavs really was. St. Augustine said, in allusion to the attraction which Manichæanism once possessed for him, that its "*imagery* put into marked contrast before him the 'most lucid substance of God,' and evil, as having its own foul and hideous bulk, whether gross, which they called earth, or thin and subtle like the body of the air."—"All dualistic religions," maintains Professor Mozley, "contain their main appeal to human reason in the circumstance of their pretension to represent facts. This is a mixed world, and it must have a mixed Deity. That is their real basis. In what form they do this—whether under the form of two gods, a good and an evil,—or of a god who is a mixture of both good and evil, or who is devoid of either, is a subordinate point."[1]

How vivid was the "imagery" of the Slavonic duality theory we have had an opportunity of observing. Every force in nature, as well as every occurrence in daily life, was pressed into the service of one or other of the two great conflicting principles, which were supposed to be engaged in an unending struggle for the empire of the universe. In the faintest breeze that stirred the leaves into a whisper, in the lightest cloud that sailed across the blue, in the most careless twitter of the waking bird at sunrise, there lurked a meaning, a message, of good or evil import, from the

[1] 'The Manichæans and the Jewish Fathers,' in Prof. Mozley's 'Ruling Ideas in Early Ages,' pp. 258, 259.

D

other world. How much more in the appalling manifestations of nature ;—in the muttering thunder and the writhing lightning, in winds that awoke groans in the forests, and earthquakes that shook the very hills !

Between the people and the mystic domains of the supernatural—the theatre of that incomprehensible battle of the gods—stood the priests.

In them was vested a power which, outside the sacred circle of the hierarchy, was nowhere to be found.

They knew how to gratify, and how to draw down blessings from the good spirits. And how—more important still,—to avoid and hinder the deadly shafts of the evil ones. To them the book of nature, which others might not decipher, was written in legible characters.[1] And when we remember what "nature" was to the Slavonic races, even long after other nations had learnt to look beyond her to the God Who made her, we cannot wonder that no bounds checked the credulity, the awe, the obedience, commanded by the priesthood. "The earliest historical ideal of heathendom," it has been thoughtfully remarked, "is the worship of physical strength : it finds its peculiar sphere in the Asiatic continent. Mr. Buckle, in his history of European civilization,

---

[1] "When Deity is revealed only in nature, one cannot be oblivious of the fact that nature in her parts is to a certain degree in man's power, and in all countries men have believed that there are means, known to the initiated, of increasing that power a hundred or a thousand fold ; so that a polytheistic worship of God in nature easily degenerates, without losing its æsthetic charm, into the celebration of real or supposed magical incantations," &c.—'Foregleams of Christianity,' p. 38. .

has mentally divided the human race into two great sections : in the one, man has power over nature ; in the other, nature has power over man. The former is the characteristic of Europe, the latter of Asia. We believe the distinction to be at once historical and philosophical. As we survey the great systems of Asiatic worship, we are impressed, beyond all other things, with the conviction that we are in the presence of a life where the aspect of nature is more reverenced than the movements of mind, where the individual sinks into insignificance in the contemplation of an outward universe, whose vast extent and changeless duration contrast so painfully with the frailty of his human years."

"The outward universe appeared invulnerable by time, and it was therefore an object of reverence ; the individual life was transitory and fading, and it was therefore an object of contempt." [1]

The Christian ideal was "the antagonist and the subversion of the worship of physical power. So far from being created by that worship, it could only begin to exist in its decay and death. It grew out of another order of thought,—it was the product of a contrary element, and the element which produced it was foreign, not only to the mind of Judea, but to the entire genius of the Asiatic intellect." [2]

We find the heathen Slavonians, then, prostrated before their altars of propitiation, their piteous gaze

---

[1] "The Originality of the Character of Christ."—*Contem-porary Review*, Nov. 1878.
[2] Ibid.

riveted on the distant portals of the unseen, to which their priests jealously guarded the passage. By what they saw and understood not, they judged of what they did not see.

Far off, as yet, were the feet of those who were bringing good tidings, and publishing peace.[1] Slowly would the timid and desponding Slavonians be brought to believe the news they carried, for it was soothing, and not alarming. But to them, too, fearful as they were, the message of the perfect Love, Which casteth out fear, was on its way, and in this desert, also, a highway was to be "made strait" for God.

[1] In one respect, at least, the missionaries, when they did arrive, avoided creating unnecessary prejudice. They did not present the God Whose worship they advocated under any strange name. On the contrary, they contented themselves with adopting the general term for "deity" in the Slavonic tongue, i.e. *Bog* or *Bogu.* Considering the indiscreet intolerance, and the abhorrence of the Slavonic language, on the score of which the story, as it progresses, will oblige us to find these missionaries for the most part blameworthy, this circumstance deserves recollection.

CHAPTER III.

THE CONVERSION OF BULGARIA.

"The name of the Bulgarians," writes Dean Milman, "a race, next to the Huns, the most terrible and most hateful to the invaded Europeans, was known in the West as early as the reign of Theodoric the Ostrogoth. Either mingled with, or bordering upon, the Slavonians, they spread over a large tract of territory, from the shores of the Palus Mæotis and the Euxine, along the course of the Lower Danube." [1]

This people appears to have been "of Asiatic origin, of the same stock with the Huns." [2] Towards the close of the 7th century, they attacked and conquered the division of the Slavs settled in Mœsia, and, in the first instance, gave their own name to the tribes they had subdued. In the course of two centuries, however, having adopted the language and manners of the Slavonians, the conquerors became identified with their subjects. [3]

The precise position of their very earliest haunts is a somewhat vexed question. It is held by many that their primeval home was on the banks of the Volga, and that this river either owed its name to the Bul-

---

[1] 'Latin Christianity,' ii. 418.
[2] Robertson's ' History of the Christian Church,' iii. 431.
[3] See Krasinski's Lectures [Ed. 1851]. p. 20, note.

garians, or bestowed it upon them.[1] This opinion,
however, has been warmly combated.[2]

The Bulgarians are said to have originally sprung
from a Turanian stock. But "in the latter decades
of the 4th century, the populations belonging to the
three great Teutonic, Slavonic, and Turanian—or
Mongol—races, had become intermingled, and, so to
speak, interlaced with each other, by the action of
war and migration."[3]

In order to lay before the reader an outline of the
characteristics to be expected in a people of Turanian
birth, a passage, from the author to whom appeal has
just been made, is here transcribed, which bears
upon the attributes of the *Huns*. For they, as far as
Turanian extraction was concerned, were of kin to
the Bulgarians.[4]

"The Huns," then, "are fickle, faithless, change-
able as the wind ; a prey to the furious impulse of
the moment ; they know no more than brute beasts
the distinction between right and wrong. As for
religion, or religious instinct, they have none, nor do

---

[1] Milman [Ed. 1854], ii. 418.

[2] See *The Athenæum*, No. 2664, p. 620.

[3] 'Nationalities,' p. 176. "The terms *Turanian* and *Mongol*
are not exactly identical, for Dr. Latham has observed that as a
linguistic appellative the former has a larger range ; whereas in
anthropology the second is the wider class."—'Nationalities,' 147.

[4] "The Huns will serve for us as an ethnological type of all
those tribes of Turanian stock—Avars, Bulgarians, Turks—who
appeared, each with more appalling aspect than the other, from
behind the Ural mountains and the Caspian Sea, on the frontiers
of the falling Empire."—'Nationalities,' p. 148.

they practise any form of worship. Gold is the object of their passionate adoration. They surpass in barbarism and ferocity all that we can conceive, of barbarous and ferocious."[1] This is the testimony of Ammianus Marcellinus, and bears date about the year A.D. 375.

Of the Finns, again, also of Turanian parentage, Tacitus speaks, as a "marvellously savage race," having "neither arms, horses, nor household gods; their food is herbage, their clothing, skins; their sleeping-place, the bare ground; their only hope of sustenance rests in their arrows, which, from want of iron, they point with bones."

The Turanians of the remotest antiquity, it is true, offer a curiously marked contrast to the above unattractive picture. It is well known to be the opinion of many modern writers of note, that the authors of the Cuneiform inscriptions which of late years have excited such great and general interest, were of none other than Turanian origin. This belief does but corroborate the views of the Roman historian Trogus Pompeius, which were based upon an ancient tradition that the Turanian race was the first to acquire the advanced scientific knowledge and elaborate culture of a highly developed civilization.[2]

[1] 'Nationalities,' pp. 150, 152.
[2] "Un passage célèbre de l'historien Justin," writes M. Lenormant, "dit qu'antérieurement à la puissance de toute autre nation, l'Asie des anciens, l'Asie antérieure, fut en entier possédée pendant quinze siècles par les Scythes, c'est-à-dire par les Touraniens, dont il fait le plus vieux peuple du monde,

In the valley of the Tigris and the Euphrates, it would appear, this condition of social and intellectual enlightenment chiefly flourished. The Accadians[1] of Babylonia, however, probably succumbed to the Hamitic Cushites about the year B.C. 3500. Not long after this, " the inhabitants of Babylonia were familiar with scientifically constructed buildings, gem-engraving, metal-work in gold, silver, bronze, and iron, bas-reliefs and sculptures in the round, embroidered dresses, elegant furniture, the art of writing, mathematical science—including the knowledge of square and cube roots, an elaborate system of weights and measures, treatises on various sciences, regular laws, extensive commerce and ship-building, artificial irrigation, scientific tillage of the ground, &c. It is hardly rash, moreover, to conclude that these inventions were in the main of Turanian origin, as we know from the records of another Turanian nation, which has never been overwhelmed by any other race, and

plus ancien même que les Egyptiens. Cette donnée, que Trogue-Pompée avait puisée dans les traditions asiatiques, est aujourd'hui confirmée par les découvertes de la science, et passe à l'état de vérité fondée sur des preuves solides. Le résultat le plus considérable et le plus inattendu des études assyriologiques a été la révélation du développement des populations touraniennes dans toute l'Asie antérieure avant les Aryas et les Sémites, et de la part prépondérante qu'elles eurent à la naissance des premières civilisations de cette partie de monde."
—'Les premières Civilisations.'

[1] The *Accadian* was " the aboriginal element in the population of Babylonia, Assyria, Susiana, and Armenia."—'Fore-gleams of Christianity,' Appendix, p. 217. " The magic of Jews and Gnostics, of mediæval sorcerers and witches, can all be traced to the superstitions of the primitive population of Accad."
—'Babylonian Literature,' Rev. A. H. Sayce, M.A., p. 49.

which has carefully preserved its chronicles, how familiar were the Chinese with similar arts and sciences —at least the real Chinese, ' the hundred families'— not long after, and probably before, their settlement in the far East of the Asiatic continent." [1]   But with reference to the religious aspect of the subject, it may be observed, finally, that about the year B.C. 2000, Sargon, king of Aganê, is believed to have reigned over the whole of Babylonia, and that although—supposing this date to be correct—1500 years must have elapsed since the Cushites had sub-dued the aborigines, no regular priesthood had been established in the valley of the Tigris and the Euphrates until his time.   " The Accadians, who were then permitted to form an inferior order of the Chal-dæan caste, were not priests, but magicians." [2]

But to return to Bulgaria.

"How early the Bulgarians became *Slavonized*," says Dr. Latham, " we cannot tell.   Nor can we give the details of the Bulgarian kingdom on its origin. We only know that during the prevalence of the Hun name, that of the Bulgarian was unknown ; and that soon after the break-up of the kingdom of Attila, the word 'Bulgarian' presents itself.   As a rule, they are the enemies of the Empire ; and, as a rule, they are allied with the Slavonians." [3] It should be borne in mind that these Bulgarians

---

[1] 'Foregleams of Christianity,' pp. 114, 115.

[2] Ibid., p. 117. But varying opinions are held with respect to these dates. Mr. Sayce speaks of Aganê as "a city near Sippara, founded by Sargon I., probably in the 17th century B.C."—'Babylonian Literature,' p. 9.

[3] 'Russian and Turk,' p. 133.

could not, however gradually, become blended with the defeated Slavonians of Mœsia without importing among them some, at least, of their own peculiar characteristics. Enough has been said to show that such importations could not have been otherwise than most unpromising.

The conversion of Bulgaria is our present theme. And it is advisable to remember that the uninviting elements of Turanian character, above specified, —even if considerably modified, or, indeed, only reflected,—were anything but hopeful ingredients for the construction of a Christian community. For, in order to judge accurately of the upspringing of seed sown,—fairly to estimate its slow or rapid fructification, its interrupted or its successful growth,—some knowledge of the soil which received it is imperatively necessary.

Reasonable expectations of progress of any kind can be based only on a thorough acquaintance with attendant circumstances, and the obstacles which lay heaped in the several paths of early Christianity are often too little taken into account. Let us borrow the noble thought of a modern writer of note, on this call for careful comparison of capabilities and achievement, nor reject his words as inapplicable, because they refer to physical life in its humblest forms, and not to things confessedly spiritual. For, as in a glass,—and less and less darkly as our gaze becomes more earnest,—we may behold in the ways of Nature lessons of grace.

" It would be hard upon a plant, if, after being tied to a particular spot,—where it is indeed much wanted,

and is a great blessing, but where it has enough to do
to live,—whence it cannot move to obtain what it needs
or likes, but must stretch its unfortunate arms here
and there for bare breath and light, and *split its way
among rocks*, and grope for sustenance in unkindly
soil,—it would be hard, I say, if, under all these dis-
advantages, it were made answerable for its appearance, and found fault with, because it was not a fine
plant of the kind. That is always an ideal oak,
which, however poverty-stricken, or hunger-pinched,
or tempest-tortured, is yet seen to have done, under
its appointed circumstances, all that could be expected of oak."[1]

The Bulgarians were a perennial source of disquiet
to the Greek emperors. On the particulars of the
many fierce inroads[2] in which they took either a leading or a subordinate part, it is not to our purpose to
dwell.

In the year A.D. 775, Constantine V. died, " be-
queathing to his successors the coercion of the Bulgarians as a condition of the security of the northern
provinces of his empire. Their power, however, though
more than once broken, was never annihilated, until
the time of the Ottomans. Soon after the establishment of the Avar dominion, and after the breaking up
of the power of Attila,[3] the Bulgarian kingdom of
Krum, Bogoris, and their pagan predecessors, began.

[1] Ruskin's 'Modern Painters,' ii. p. 103.
[2] Gibbon, v. pp. 231, 329, 331.
[3] Dr. Latham's 'Native Races of the Russian Empire,'
p. 254.

By this time, the whole land, whatever it may have been before, is Slavonic." [1]

The allusion just made to the *Avars*, suggesting the period of their dominance as an approximate starting-point for the Bulgarian kingdom, leads us to the passing remark that the name *Avar* has been often confusedly applied both to the original Asiatic proprietors of it, and to certain neighbouring tribes,— the "Ouars," or *Khouni* [χοῦνοι], whom they reduced to submission. This appellation, χοῦνοι, was bestowed by the Greek historians on the Huns.   These Ouar Khouni it was, who, flying themselves from the thraldom of the Turks, first precipitated themselves on the Empire in the middle of the 6th century, under the terror-inspiring name of the *Avars*.[2]   According to the patriarch Nicholaos, writing in the year A.D. 807, this powerful race had then kept possession of the Peloponnesus for 218 years, and had so completely separated it from the Byzantine empire, that no Byzantine official dared to put his foot in the country." " There is good reason," Dr. Latham observes, " for attaching great hosts of Slavonians" to the Avar armies.[3]   He takes " the history of the *Slavonizers of Hellas*" to have " begun with that of the Avars, continued with that of the Bulgarians, and ended with the amalgamation of the invaders with the older occupiers of the land." [4]

---

[1] Dr. Latham's ' Russian and Turk,' p. 134.
    See Sheppard's ' Nationalities,' p. 212.
[3] ' Russian and Turk,' p. 146. See also Gibbon [Smith's edition, 1854], v. 171.
[4] ' Russian and Turk,' p. 148.

It has been thought that the origin of the word
Morea is Slavonic, and in support of this view it is
urged that the Byzantine writers never speak of the
Peloponnesus by that name, the inference being that
its derivation was barbaric. For no repugnance would,
presumably, have been evinced by Greek authors to a
word of Greek extraction. But whether we detect
in the sea-girt "*Morea*" traces of the Slavonic *more*,
the Sea,—or content ourselves with the popular idea
of the mulberry-leaf, we must accept the witness of
Cedrenus, of Theophanes, and of the patriarch Nicephorus, who wrote in the 8th century, to the Slavonic
presence in Greece at that time. They all call "the
country from the Danube to the highlands of Arcadia
and Messenia, *Sclabinia; i.e.,* the country of the
Slavi." Constantine Porphyrogenitus states that in
the middle of the 8th century "the whole of the
Peloponnesus was Slavonized and barbarized." It is
in one of the records of this writer, that we find a
King of Bulgaria first mentioned.[1] "Many locali-
ties described by Pausanias, and even by Procopius,
have disappeared, and have been replaced by others,
bearing Slavonic names; as *Goritza, Slavitza, Velogisti,*
&c."[2]

In the year A.D. 811, the emperor Nicephorus,
highly incensed by the arrogance and hostility of the
Bulgarians, marched into their territory, and destroyed

[1] The first Bulgarian kingdom, according to Dr. Latham,
began about A.D. 640, and ended, A.D. 1017.—'Native Races,'
p. 254.

[2] Krasinski's Lectures [1851]. Appendix, p. 331.

the palace of their king by fire. Three days only
elapsed before this indignity was amply avenged.
The enraged Bulgarians fell upon the emperor and
slew him, together with his principal officers. After
parading the imperial head tauntingly on a spear,
the savage warriors converted the skull into a drinking-
bowl, which they ornamented with gold enrichments,
and from it they were accustomed to quaff their deep
draughts of triumph on the occasion of their wildest
revelries. It is plain that their early instincts were
as yet by no means weakened.

But after a while, a ray of light pierced the darkness. It glanced from behind prison bars.

In the beginning of this 9th century, a sister of the
reigning Bulgarian king, Bogoris, had fallen as a
captive into the keeping of the Greek emperor.
For thirty-eight years she lived at Constantinople,
and was there instructed in the doctrines of the
Christian Faith.

Meanwhile, the administration passed into the hands
of the empress Regent, Theodora. She was interested
in a certain monk named Cupharas, who had been
taken prisoner by the Bulgarians, and with a view
to his redemption, she opened negotiations with
Bogoris. An exchange of prisoners was finally effected.
The sister of Bogoris was restored to him, while
Cupharas was permitted to return to Constantinople.

Before the release of the pious monk, however, he
had striven, though quite unavailingly, to win the
Bulgarian prince to the service of the Cross. These

fruitless endeavours were supplemented by the entreaties of the king's sister, on her return from Constantinople. But even to such a suppliant Bogoris
turned a deaf ear.

At last, fear snapped the fetters which love had
failed to disengage. A famine,—or, as some say, a
pestilence,—occurred, and the anxieties of the king
were aroused. In vain he petitioned his own deities
for relief. None came. The scourge which so distressed him continued to afflict his country. In these
straits, he at length consented to invoke the God Whom
his sister worshipped ; nor were his tardy prayers
unanswered. The grievous visitation was suspended,
and the proud spirit of the pagan prince bowed low
before the Author and Giver of all good things.

But he had slender hope of inducing his subjects
to share his new-born convictions.

His baptism was celebrated at midnight with
profoundest secrecy. The rite was administered
by no less a personage than the patriarch Photius.
He emphasized the solemnity of the occasion by
presenting the neophyte with a lengthy treatise on
Christianity, theoretical and practical, considered
mainly in its bearings on the duties of a monarch.
The emperor Michael stood sponsor by proxy, and
the Bulgarian king received, as his Christian name,
that of his imperial godfather.[1]

Two monks of note were at this time living at Constantinople. They were the sons of one Leon—or

---

[1] Robertson's 'History of the Christian Church,' iii. 431.

Leo—of Thessalonica. Both were men of mark, each in his own department of culture. Cyril, otherwise called Constantine, was a linguist, for his day. He was familiar with the Greek, Latin, Slavonian, Armenian, and Khasarian languages. Methodius, the other brother, was a painter of no mean skill.[1] In monasteries only, the art of the period found a home.

Solicited by Bogoris for the services of a painter competent to decorate his palace, the emperor despatched Methodius to the Bulgarian court.

The king, true to the leanings of his race, directed the monk, on his arrival, to embellish the walls of the royal entrance-hall with a series of terrifying pictures. Instead of turning to the chase or the battle-field for subjects, Methodius executed the behests of his patron by painting the awful scenes of the " Last Judgment." Bogoris, gazing at the frightful doom of the heathen, as depicted by the pious artist, shuddered at the spectacle, and forthwith abandoned the idols with which he had hitherto found himself unable to part. Nor were the dreadful pictures effectless upon his courtiers. Many of them participated to such an extent in their master's agitation, that they became candidates for admission into the Christian Church.

But the bulk of his subjects remained devotedly pagan, and when the secret of his baptism at last transpired, they cast their allegiance

---

[1] Milman's 'Latin Christianity' [Ed. 1854], ii. 420.'

to the winds, menaced the king with death, and attacked his palace. This heathen demonstration, however, did not alarm Bogoris. He marched boldly, with no large force, against the rebels, wearing the Cross upon his breast. That holy symbol, indeed, was quite out of keeping with the merciless punishment inflicted by him upon the insurgents, who quailed before his resolute aspect. Nevertheless, a line was drawn between the plebeians among the offenders, and the men of high degree who had instigated them to revolt. These nobles, with their entire families, were put to death, while pardon was extended to the lower orders.

Bogoris did not long rest satisfied with half-measures. He began to revolve in his mind projects for the conversion of the Bulgarians as a nation. But on pondering the formulas tendered to him by Photius at his baptism, he found them far too exalted for his comprehension. More perplexed than edified by these written arguments which he could not follow, he was further confounded by the rival exhortations of sundry missionaries who had found their way into Bulgaria.

These zealots were the exponents of differing creeds—Greek, Roman, Armenian—and each naturally pressed his favourite dogmas on the royal acceptance. Distracted by such conflicting pretensions, and also prompted, possibly, by an unspoken dread of the Greek Empire, whose shadow lay almost across his kingdom, Bogoris determined to go straight to the fountain-head.

He therefore applied to Pope Nicolas I. for advice

E

as to matters of faith. He is said to have submitted no less than 106 questions to the pontiff for solution. These embraced, as well they might, "every point of ecclesiastical discipline, of ceremonial observance, and of manners."[1]

The appeal was far from unavailing. The pope adapted himself with considerable adroitness to the difficulties of this untutored son of the Church. The contents of his voluminous despatch to Bogoris deserve our careful attention.

Mildly rebuking the Bulgarian king for the barbarity with which he had recently treated his rebellious subjects, and pointing out that at his baptism he had enrolled himself under a standard emblazoned with mercy, and not with violence, the august director proceeded to deprecate the employment of force in the promulgation of the Faith. It might indeed, he said, be well to withdraw from communion with persistent idolaters, but persuasion should on every possible occasion take precedence of stronger measures. To this rule of toleration, the case of apostates constituted the solitary exception. To the grievous sin of relapse leniency was not enjoined.

Nicolas was astute enough to accommodate his injunctions, within certain limits, to the fierce and undisciplined nature of the people for whom he was legislating. He perceived that, there being no hope as yet of quenching the Bulgarian passion for war, his present efforts must be directed only to brid-

---

[1] 'Latin Christianity' [Ed. 1854], ii. 421.

ling, guiding, and chastening it. The national ensign was no longer to be the time-honoured horse-tail, but the Cross itself. The Bulgarian warriors were advised at once and for ever to abjure enchantments and all kindred pagan superstitions, and to consecrate their war sallies by solemn, dedicatory attendance at church, by confessing their sins, offering alms, and doing charitable deeds.

It had been the Bulgarian custom, on the eve of battle, to subject the horse and accoutrements of every soldier to a searching inspection; if in any case they were found to fall below the appointed standard of efficiency, the owner was unhesitatingly put to death. Availing himself of this practice as a text, the pope recommended that henceforth the thorough *spiritual* equipment of each warrior should rather be the object of solicitude.

Oaths were to be in future administered on the Holy Gospels, and not, as heretofore, on the characteristic sword driven into the ground. Polygamy was declared to be inadmissible, but Bogoris was gently admonished to be courteous to his queen, who had hitherto been kept at so respectful a distance, that she neither dined with her husband nor sat down in his presence. In urging the prince to cultivate the grace of humility, Nicolas did not fail to point to the Great Exemplar, Who condescended to associate and to eat with the lowliest. Bogoris had anxiously inquired whether intercessory prayer might be offered for his pagan ancestors. But this was peremptorily orbidden. Nor did the pope accede to his request that a patriarch might be appointed to Bulgaria. Before taking such a step, he must, he said, receive the report of his episcopal envoys, whom he now sent among the Bulgarians. These were Paul, bishop of Populonia, and Formosus, bishop of Portus, both of whom were the bearers of Bibles and other books of spiritual instruction. Pending the regular organization of the Bulgarian Church, whose members were as yet not even numbered, the question of a patriarch must be left in abeyance.

Besides, argued Nicolas, there were in reality only three true patriarchal sees, for those of apostolic foundation could alone be recognized as genuine. This observation was intended to exclude Jerusalem and Constantinople from the honours of the patriarchate. The papal letter concluded with adjurations to loyalty to the Roman Church, mingled with disapproving remarks upon some of the usages of the Greek communion.

Simultaneously with his suit to the pope, Bogoris had made an appeal for religious enlightenment to the Western emperor, Louis of Germany. Louis is said to have furnished him, by way of response, with a bishop. This prelate, however, finding the ground occupied by the papal envoys, seems to have returned home without taking any action.[1]

The religious affairs of Bulgaria were not destined to be peacefully settled by the pastoral letter of Pope Nicolas. No sooner did the news reach Constanti-

---

[1] Robertson, iii. 434.

nople that Western influence had been brought to bear upon the kingdom of Bogoris, than the wrath of the Byzantine patriarch was violently inflamed. He insisted that, as the seeds of Christianity had been implanted in Bulgaria by Byzantine hands, and had ripened, in the baptism of the king, under Greek auspices, the Bulgarians belonged by right to the fold of the Oriental Church. Nicolas, on the other hand, rejoined that before Bulgaria was wrested from the Empire by its present possessors, it had pertained to the Roman jurisdiction,—that, moreover, the king had voluntarily applied to him for help and instruction, and that as he had provided the required instrumentality in the shape of clergy and churches, the credit of the conversion of the kingdom as a kingdom, whatever might be said about individuals, certainly could only be his. Photius, however, disdained the papal representations. He angrily summoned a council at Constantinople, and in a circular letter to the patriarchs of Alexandria, Antioch, and Jerusalem, he inveighed bitterly against the encroachments of Rome. By the intrusive energies of the Latin Church, his people, he complained, were in danger of doctrinal corruption. Mischievous innovations were introduced, both with respect to fasting, to celibacy, to the second unction, and other kindred points, and also to the important question of the Procession of the Spirit. The departure from orthodoxy on this last subject was the chief offence. The patriarch vehemently appealed against the Roman tenet to the authority of Athanasius, Gregory, and Basil, and denouncing

Rome herself as Antichrist, he invited his correspon-
dents to despatch representatives to Constantinople.
A combined resistance to Latin pretensions might in
this way, he thought, be organized without delay.
The tone of his present letter, be it observed,
harmonized very imperfectly with the spirit of the
memorable treatise bestowed by him on Bogoris at
his baptism.

The challenge of Photius echoed, of course, through
the Christian world. Papal apologists promptly came
to the front. The accusations of the patriarch were
hotly repelled by Hincmar, archbishop of Rheims,
Odo, bishop of Beauvais, Æneas of Paris, and Rat-
ramnus of Corbey. Thus the battle-cries of theology
rang over Christendom, and the world was regaled
with the spectacle of a struggle between the rival
Churches for the possession of Bulgaria, a country
till recently so conspicuously destitute of dogma of
any kind. The Bulgarians themselves, doubtless much
astonished at the uproar for their sake, and, surely,
more perplexed than ever by the manners and customs
of Christianity, began to waver in their adherence to the
Western Church, and to exhibit symptoms of an inclination to transfer their allegiance to Constantinople.
The strife went on for years. At last, A.D. 877, the
Latin clergy having been dismissed from the country,
Pope John VIII. solemnly expostulated, protesting
against the Greek proclivities of the Bulgarians, and
predicting dire results from their identity with a
Church which was rarely free from heresy in one
form or another.

Nevertheless, the Byzantine leanings of Bulgaria did culminate in union with the Eastern Church. A Greek archbishop, and bishops of the same communion, settled in the country. Photius had, meanwhile, been deposed as an usurper, and Ignatius, whom he had displaced, formally reinstated. But Ignatius, though he had acknowledged the papal authority,[1] was not more disposed than Photius had been, to relinquish Bulgaria. He, indeed, consecrated the archbishop already mentioned. But he was threatened with deposition, as well as excommunication, if he did not loosen his grasp on the much-coveted country. He owed his dignified position—said the voice from the pontifical chair—to the papal see, and he must forfeit it, or cede Bulgaria to the Western Church. How Ignatius might have treated these solemn utterances, had his life been spared, it is impossible to guess. His death, which occurred that very year, put an end to the contention. But it was soon revived in the person of Photius, who, for the second time, ascended to the vacant seat of Ignatius. He inaugurated his new elevation by the convention of a synod at Constantinople, at which he invited the attendance of papal legates. Hastily construing this overture into a preliminary to the relinquishment of Bulgaria, Pope John accepted the invitation. His emissaries were charged to convey the papal pardon, on certain conditions, to Photius, whose humble frame of mind he took entirely for granted. They were

[1] Robertson, iii. p. 440.

instructed to resist to the uttermost all claims to Bulgaria on the part of the patriarch.[1] On their arrival at Constantinople, however, they discovered that the pontiff's conclusions had been prematurely drawn, and coloured by his ardent wishes. Photius displayed perfect independence of spirit, repudiating all assumption that he required any extension of the papal sceptre, and steadily putting aside the Bulgarian question as irrelevant to the topics proposed for debate.

Foiled where he had least expected it, Pope John had no consolation except in his own anger, which escaped in copious anathemas, hurled furiously at the obdurate patriarch.

Three succeeding popes took up the quarrel, and made it their own.

And here we must leave Bulgaria, the apple of discord among these venerable personages for so many years. The dawn of Christianity in other kingdoms claims our observation.

But we may state, in withdrawing from Bulgarian ground, that in the year A.D. 923, king Symeon, while prescribing terms of a peace to be concluded with the emperor Romanus I., stipulated for the acknowledgment of the chief Bulgarian bishop by Constantinople, as an independent patriarch; "and this lasted until John Tzimisces put an end to the Bulgarian kingdom, A.D. 972."[2]

---

[1] A.D. 879.
[2] Finlay, ii. 81, quoted by Robertson, iii. 449 [note].

The conversion of Bulgaria led to the extension of Christian influences in other quarters,[1] counteracted though they were, in several cases, by the proselytizing exertions of Jews and Mussulmans.

[1] Notably in the Crimea, the interior of Hellas, Servia, &c.

CHAPTER IV.

THE CONVERSION OF MORAVIA, BOHEMIA, AND SERVIA.

THE geographical confines of ancient Moravia, which was far from an insignificant kingdom, must not be confused with those of the modern province which has inherited its name. In the opening years of the 9th century, Moravia stretched from the Bavarian borders to the Hungarian river Drina,[1] and from the banks of the Danube, beyond the Carpathian mountains, to the river Stryi[2] in Southern Poland.

Into this territory Christianity had been ushered as early as A.D. 801, by Charlemagne, who, as his custom was, enforced baptism at the point of the sword, at least as far as the king was concerned. Efforts were subsequently made by the archbishops of Salzburg and Passau to fan this first feeble flicker into something like a flame. But no success attended their exertions. Paganism was overpoweringly strong, and Christianity not only weak, but rude and uncouth in type. The native princes, unattracted by solemnities conducted in a language unintelligible to them, soon sank back into heathenism, and the spark of light, ceasing to struggle with the heavy atmosphere, expired.

But in the year A.D. 863, the Moravian king Ros-

[1] See Krasinski, p. 20 [Ed. 1851].   [2] Ibid.

tislav,[1] anxious to shake off the yoke of the Western Empire, sought to strengthen his hands by a political alliance with Michael, the Greek emperor. He accordingly commissioned ambassadors to solicit the imperial co-operation, and it is said that his nephew Sviatopolk, who was one of the envoys, became a convert to Christianity while absent on this mission.[2]

On his return to Moravia, Sviatopolk called the king's attention to the new creed, and was warmly seconded in his advocacy of its claims, by the queen, herself already a professing Christian. Their efforts resulted in a formal application to the emperor Michael on the part of king Rostislav, for teachers qualified to expound Christianity in the Slavonic tongue.

Bogoris had appealed to the pope,—Rostislav importuned the emperor; one turned to the West, the other stretched out his hands to the East, for help; but in both cases it was a pathetic cry out of gross darkness for a share in the Great Light.

"The land is baptized," pleaded the Moravian king, "but we have no teachers to instruct us and translate for us the Sacred Books. We do not understand either the Greek or the Latin tongue,—some teach us one thing, and some another; therefore we do not understand the meaning of the Scriptures, neither their import. Send us teachers who can explain to us the words of the Scripture, and their meaning." When this petition reached the Byzantine court, the emperor lost no time in communi-

---

[1] Sometimes called Radislav.
[2] Robertson's 'History of the Christian Church,' iii. 458.

cating its tenor to his philosophers, and requesting their advice. These sages reminded their master of the two sons of Leon the Thessalonian, of whose proficiency in art and languages we have already heard. Men of such culture and piety seemed to them peculiarly qualified for evangelistic work. According to one account, indeed, Rostislav had especially begged that Cyril, one of these noted brothers, might be appointed to the Moravian mission.

A slight allusion has been made on an earlier page, to the rise of Christianity among the Chazars of the Ukraine and the Crimea. Eighteen years before the errand of Methodius to Bulgaria, these tribes, finding themselves unable to discriminate between the contradictory claims of Judaism, Mahometanism, and Christianity, had reported their difficulties at Constantinople, accompanying the statement with an entreaty for assistance : A.D. 843.

Constantine—better known under the name of Cyril, which he is said to have assumed towards the end of his life, in obedience to a vision,[1]—was the chosen apostle to the Chazars. His labours among them were crowned with remarkable success. He declined any compensation for himself, stipulating only for the release of all Christian captives in the country.

On the shores of the Tauric Chersonese he had lighted upon a saintly relic, reputed to be the body

---

[1] Robertson, iii. 458.

of St. Clement. Rival remains of this saint no doubt existed in other places, but Cyril considered his particular treasure to be genuine on the ground that St. Clement, according to report, had been banished to the Chersonese by the emperor Trajan.

We return now to Constantinople, whither Cyril and Methodius repaired at the imperial summons, to hear and to act upon the Moravian appeal. " Being persuaded by the emperor," says Nestor, " they went into the Slavonic land, to Rostislav, to Sviatopolk, and to Kotzel; and, having arrived, they began to compose a Slavonic alphabet, and translated the Gospels and the Acts of the Apostles ; and the Slavonians rejoiced, hearing the greatness of God in their own language : after which they translated the Psalter and other books."

The Slavonic alphabet constructed by Cyril and Methodius consisted of the Greek letters, with some additional Armenian and Hebrew characters, besides a few signs of their own invention. "The Eastern branch" of the Slavonic languages, properly so called, " comprehends the *Russian*, with various local dialects, the *Bulgarian*, and the *Illyrian*. The most ancient document of this Eastern branch is the so-called ecclesiastical Slavonic, *i.e.*, the ancient Bulgarian, into which Cyrillus and Methodius translated the Bible in the middle of the 9th century. This is still the authorized version of the Bible for the whole Slavonic race, and to the student of the Slavonic languages it is what Gothic is to the student of German. The *modern* Bulgarian, on the contrary, as far as grammatical forms are concerned, is the most reduced among the Slavonic dialects."[1]

The importance of the service rendered by these indefatigable missionaries, in translating the Scriptures into the native language, cannot be overestimated.

When the champions of a new and unknown faith have to disarm prejudice and to enchain attention, no method can compete for a moment with the policy of clothing the unaccustomed tenets in the accents of that tongue with which the peasant has been familiar from his cradle. How uncouth and unmusical soever its cadences may sound in other ears, they have a power all their own to unlock his heart and enlist his affections. Where one language is for things human, and another for things divine, the priest may appeal, but he will appeal in vain, to the sympathies of the people. In the foreign tongue a line—fatal to the growth of spiritual life—has been drawn, and cannot be overstepped, between the visible and the Invisible, the apparent and the Real, the shadow and the Substance, the "here" and the Hereafter. Two lives, the earthly and the unearthly, which should act and react upon one another, have been divided, and can be re-united only by one bridge, —the homely language of home. But to this truth hierarchical instinct has been too seldom friendly.

" In every country converted by the Latin Church, the Scriptures and the Liturgy had been introduced,"

[1] Prof. Max Müller's ' Science of Language,' i. 205.

as we know on an authority which is second to none, "not in the vernacular language of the original or conquered population, but in the language of the government or missionaries, the Latin language of the old Empire and the new Church of Rome. Our own sense and experience are sufficient to tell us what a formidable obstacle must have been created by this single cause to the mutual and general understanding of the new faith ; what barriers between the conquerors and conquered, between the educated and the vulgar, above all, between the clergy and the laity. In the Eastern Church, on the other hand, a contrary method was everywhere followed. The same principle which had led Jerome, in his cell at Bethlehem, to translate the Bible into what was then the one known language of the West, was adopted by the Oriental Church with regard to all the nations that came within its sphere. Hence, in the remote East, sprang up the Syriac, Coptic, Armenian, and Ethiopic versions ; hence, in the only attempt made by the Eastern Church on the Western barbarians, Ulfilas immortalized himself by producing the only wide-spread translation of the Scriptures which existed in any Western language till the times of Wycliffe. In like manner, at the approach of the Greek Church to the Slavonic nations on the shores of the Danube, the first labour of the missionaries, Cyril and Methodius, was to invent an alphabet for the yet unwritten language of the Slavonic tribes."[1]

[1] Stanley's ' Eastern Church,' pp. 309, 310.

For four years and a half the brothers worked among the Moravians, and abundant fruit rewarded their earnest toil.   Churches were built, conversions were numerous, and such respect was inspired by the missionaries, that a title was assigned to them, equivalent, in the Slavonic tongue, to *princes*.   But matters were not always to roll thus smoothly on.   Jealousies and suspicions arose among the German priests. Whispers of disparagement began to circulate, murmurs crept to and fro ; the performance of divine service in the vernacular, nay, the Slavonic alphabet itself, seemed to give great and general offence.   " Some persons," records Nestor, " began to blame the Slavonian Scriptures, saying that it does not become any nation to have its own alphabet, except the Hebrews, the Greeks, and the Latins, according to the inscription of Pilate, which he wrote on the Cross of our Lord.[1]

Rumours of the uneasiness current among the Latin clergy at last travelled to Rome.   The pope thereupon cited Cyril and Methodius to appear before him without delay, and to give account of their proceedings. This summons was immediately obeyed. The brothers started for Rome, taking the precious relics of St. Clement with them.   These remains, which had accompanied them throughout their Moravian mission, were accredited with large miraculous powers, and in Rome they produced a considerable sensation.   Pope Nicolas had died just

---

[1] ' Reformation in Poland,' Krasinski, i. 12 [note].

before the arrival of the brothers, but they were introduced to his successor, Adrian II. By him their orthodoxy was tested, and the principles on which they had conducted their work of evangelization duly examined.

The pope, declaring himself satisfied with the result of his inquiries, then consecrated Methodius archbishop of Moravia,[1] a practical acknowledgment of the independence of the Moravian Church which was very agreeable to king Rostislav. Cyril died in Rome, and was buried in the church of St. Clement. Methodius, however, returned to Moravia, his position substantially strengthened by the papal sanction. For some little time he prosecuted his labours with steadily increasing success. But again shadows fell athwart the sunshine.

Rostislav, after a protracted and ineffectual struggle against Louis of Germany, was at length betrayed by his nephew Sviatopolk into the imperial power. He was blinded, A.D. 870, by the orders of Louis, and deprived of his throne, which the treacherous Sviatopolk was permitted to occupy in his stead. Under the administration of the new king, Methodius found himself beset by difficulties. On one occasion, indeed, it is said that he was even driven to the necessity of excommunicating the sovereign.[2] The old prejudice against his Slavonic Bible and Liturgy revived, and fresh complaints of him were lodged at

---

[1] Robertson, iii. 461; Milman, ii. 427.
[2] Robertson, iii. 462.

Rome. Aspersions were now cast upon the doctrines he preached, as well as upon the language in
which they were clothed. At this time, A.D. 879, Pope
John VIII. was much occupied, as we have seen,
with the Bulgarian quarrel. It was in the August of
this year that he despatched his legates to the synod
at Constantinople, in charge of the olive branch which
he imagined the contrition of Photius to deserve.

Methodius journeyed a second time to Rome, and
presented himself to John, who engaged him in
argument; and a lengthy discussion resulted in a
compromise, the pope agreeing to sanction the use
of the Slavonic language, subject to certain conditions
and restrictions of no great importance. The story
goes, that in the course of the debate, the command
in the Psalter, "Praise the Lord, *all* ye nations,"
came home with irresistible force to the pope's mind.
If the glory of God was indeed intended to be proclaimed only in three languages, a very meagre construction must clearly be put upon this plain injunction. Other languages also must surely be referable
to the allwise Creator. The Moravian Liturgy, he
therefore decided, might be read in the vernacular,
but the mass must be celebrated either in Greek or
Latin. Moreover, as a mark of respect to venerable
custom, the Gospel must first be read in Latin, and
then in Slavonic. And further, if the king, or any
nobleman, preferred the entire service in Latin, he
might be indulged in his private chapel.[1] Thus

---

[1] Robertson, iii. 463.

mildly did Pope John deal with Methodius, whom he manifestly perceived to be irreproachable. Grave exception has been taken by some Roman writers to the permission accorded by him to the use of the vernacular in the public services of the Church. *"Il y a des hommes qui pensent que si le pape Jean VIII. avait tenu plus ferme à l'usage du Latin dans la liturgie sacrée, il aurait rendu moins facile le schisme et la perversion des nations Slavonnes."* [1]

Methodius, confirmed in his archbishopric, now returned once more to Moravia, the bearer of a letter from the pope to Sviatopolk. John informed the king that he had already consecrated one bishop to assist the primate, and desired that another ecclesiastic worthy of elevation to the episcopate should be forthwith sent to Rome, in order that a second coadjutor might be provided for him.

And now the great work was again set in motion, Methodius continuing to regard the native language as the only channel through which the hearts of the people could be reached. The shelter of papal approval, however, only heightened his unpopularity with the German clergy, who neglected no opportunity of frustrating his efforts. Sviatopolk also seems to have thrown all his influence into the Latin scale. Nor was the good archbishop free from antagonism still nearer home. The bishop first consecrated by Pope John as his assistant, became disaffected towards him, and indeed went so far as to repudiate his

---

[1] M. Rohrbacher, xii. 354. See Robertson, iii. 464 [note].

authority. The pope did his best, in at least one letter, to console Methodius under these trying circumstances. A.D. 881.

A complete release from trouble, however, was not far off. Within a few years the pious missionary died, probably in A.D. 885. The scene of his death has been laid by some at Rome, but it seems more likely that such a man remained at his post until the last. His presence, which had embodied papal patronage, once removed, the smouldering ill-feeling towards the Slavonic clergy in Moravia broke forth in action. About a year after the death of Methodius they were expelled in numbers from the country, A.D. 886, and obliged to take refuge in Bulgaria.

Fresh political disturbances followed, which ended in the subjugation of Moravia by the people known as Hunugars, Maygars, or Hungarians, A.D. 907.

These pagans suddenly inundated Christian Europe in the 10th century. In numbers apparently countless, in brutality unparalleled, in the very rudiments of common humanity wholly deficient, their onslaught acted as a tremendous and paralyzing shock to the civilized world. None knew whence they came, nor whither they were bound. Their language was unknown, and their aspect terrifying. Startled by so unexpected and unaccountable a scourge,[1] the trembling nations identified the ravages of these appalling barbarians with monstrous calamities intended to herald the approaching dissolution of the world.

---

[1] For the Hungarian inroads see Milman's 'Latin Christianity' [1854], ii. pp. 444, 445.

Henry the Fowler at last defeated the Hungarians,
A.D. 935, near Merseburg, and some twenty years
afterwards an irrecoverable blow was dealt them by
Otho the Great.

Finally, abandoning their roaming propensities, they
became stationary within the boundaries of the country
which at present bears their name. Between the
years A.D. 949 and 974, efforts were made again and
again to irradiate the spiritual darkness of these
Hungarian tribes. From time to time a voice arose,
—now from a solitary chief, himself rescued from the
prevailing degradation, and baptized, and now from
some band of unfortunate Christian captives,—plead-
ing with the wild wanderers the cause of the Crucified
One. But it was not until the year A.D. 974, that any
organized attempt was made to win them over collectively. Pope Benedict VII. then deputed Piligrin,
the bishop of Passau, to undertake the evangelization of the country. Piligrin became archbishop of
Lorch,[1] and, assisted by a small staff of clergy, he
addressed himself to the unpromising work. The
results were most disheartening. Little impression was
made until the year A.D. 997, when, in the person of
a chief called Waik, a son of Geisa, the secular arm
was uplifted in support of Christianity. He had no
sooner ascended the throne than he directed all his
energies to the establishment of the Faith.

At his baptism, by Adelbert, bishop of Prague, this
king was called Stephen.[2] His determination cowed

---

[1] Jaffé's 'Regesta Pont. Rom.,' p. 332.

[2] Pertz, 'Mon. Germ.,' xiii. 231. The bishop was at the
time on the point of starting for Prussia.

all antagonists.   He divided his kingdom into eleven
dioceses, under the supervision of the archbishop of
Gran.   He invited monks and clergy to settle in
the country; he founded schools and Benedictine
monasteries; he promoted the culture of his people
in all possible ways, and sternly bore down opposition in every quarter.   A college at Rome, and
monasteries and hospitals at Ravenna, Constantinople,
and Jerusalem, were connected with his name,[1] and
he earned, as we may easily believe, the most favourable regard of Pope Silvester II.[2]

But Stephen's successor did not share his feelings.
A reaction succeeded this period of prosperity.
Paganism reared its head again, and as late as the
middle of the 11th century Hungary was the wrestling-
ground of the old faith and the new.   Moravia,
emerging from its burial in Hungarian barbarism, was
eventually incorporated with *Bohemia*, to which kingdom our attention must now be transferred.

We find the origin of the name *Bohemia* in the *Boii*,
a Celtic race who once occupied the country.[3]   The
land was subsequently inhabited by the Marcomanni,
and after their departure to the south-west, in company
with the Goths and Alani, by the Slavonic tribes known
as the Chekhs.   As in the case of Moravia, Christianity

---

[1] Pertz, xiii. 235.   Döllinger, iii. 34.   Gieseler, iii. 463.

[2] "Such was Stephen's hospitality to pilgrims, that the
journey through Hungary came to be generally preferred to a
sea voyage by those who were bound for the Holy Land."—
Robertson, iv. 94.

[3] "*Bojohemum*, the home of the Boii, was converted into
Bohemia."—Krasinski's Lectures [1869], p. 43.

seems to have found its earliest way to Bohemia in
the wake of Charlemagne's victorious armies. With
the tribute levied on the province it is probable that
the conqueror exacted some profession of Christianity.
In the year A.D. 844, fourteen Bohemian chiefs were
baptized at Ratisbon. But in these isolated cases,
the recognition of the new faith appears to have been
little more than a politic and superficial subscription
to the creed of the German court.

About A.D. 871, duke—or prince—Borziwoi, a
pagan, paid a visit to Sviatopolk, king of Moravia.
He was received with due courtesy, but we read
that, at dinner, his host indicated the floor as
the only suitable seat for pagans. While thus
humbly accommodated, Borziwoi and his suite
attracted the notice of Methodius, whose place
the story represents to have been at the king's high
table. Turning to the group of Bohemians, he
expressed surprise and regret that they should be
placed in such a position. "If I became a Christian,"
queried the duke, from the floor, " what should I
gain thereby?" "A place," solemnly responded
Methodius, "higher than all kings and princes." If
the tale is to be credited, Borziwoi became a convert on the spot, was at once baptized, with thirty of
his attendants, and was accompanied on his return
home by a Moravian priest. His wife Ludmilla and
her two sons readily embraced Christianity, and did
what they could to promote its general reception, but
the Bohemian courtiers were by no means unanimous
in its favour. Ratislav,—or Radislav—who succeeded

Borziwoi on the throne, was a zealous defender of the faith ; and after his death Ludmilla was earnest in her endeavours to train his two sons as its champions. But their mother, Dragomira, a determined pagan, counteracted all efforts to uphold Christianity. She destroyed the churches, exiled the clergy, and murdered her pious mother-in-law, A.D. 927. Her sons, though they had been equal sharers in their grandmother's counsels, soon betrayed widely differing inclinations. Wenceslav, the elder, was deeply imbued with the principles instilled by Ludmilla. He was upright, devout, and zealous for the truth. So little did he value the distinctions of this world, that he was on the eve of laying aside his crown to assume the cowl of a monk, A.D. 936, when Boleslav, his brother, waylaid and attacked him one day, on his way to church. Wenceslav, stronger than his assailant, disarmed and overthrew him, exclaiming, "God forgive thee, brother !" But the attendants of Boleslav, coming up, supposed Wenceslav to have acted on the aggressive, and killed him. He became the patron saint of Bohemia.[1]

Boleslav, surnamed "the Cruel," who now assumed the crown, persecuted the Christians to the heart's content of his mother. On the birth of a son, however, "he was led by a strange mixture of motives to devote the child to a religious life, by way of expiation,"[2] as it was supposed, for his brother's violent death. But he did not on that account desist from waging war against Christianity. Again the clergy were banished,

Robertson, iv. 82 [note].   [2] Ibid.

churches and monasteries levelled to the ground, and the barest tolerance denied to believers.

After a lapse of fourteen years, however, the course of the heathen Boleslav was arrested. One stronger than himself interfered with a high hand. The emperor Otho I. forced him to alter his ways. The condition attached to the peace granted by imperial condescension was, that freedom of faith should be guaranteed throughout Bohemia, and that Boleslav should rebuild the churches he had destroyed.

The suffering Bohemian Church now enjoyed a respite from assault, and ten years afterwards a reaction in her favour set in, under the auspices of Boleslav II. This king, consecrated when a child, as we saw, to a religious life, amply fulfilled the promise of his youth. Justly surnamed "the Pious," he devoted himself, as soon as he had assumed the reins of government, to the extirpation of the paganism lately rampant, and left no stone unturned to further the interests of Christianity throughout his country. With the emperor's support he founded a bishopric at Prague, which was first filled by one Dietmar, a Saxon. He was succeeded by a Bohemian of high birth, who had been educated at Magdeburg, under the superintendence of archbishop Adelbert. The name of his reverend preceptor was bestowed on him at his confirmation, in the place of *Woytiech*,[1] his Bohemian appellation.

The new prelate was characterized by unflagging energy. He built churches and monasteries, and

---

[1] Or, Wogteich.

strenuously endeavoured to reform the lives of the
people. But this was up-hill work. Paganism,
though kept at bay, was still a living power. During
the period of its triumph, the evil habits fostered by
it had grown into giant barriers against any purer influence. Adelbert found that even such Christianity
as existed among the Bohemians was mixed with
pagan elements of the deadliest kind. The clergy
were steeped in gross immorality. Polygamy was
openly practised, as well as marriage within the prohibited degrees. The slave-trade throve on a general
traffic with Jewish slave-dealers in serfs and prisoners,
who were sometimes even sold for sacrificial purposes.

The bishop strove to stem the tide of sinful living.
But his temperament was all too vehement. Perceiving
that he was called upon to grapple with colossal
evils, he threw his whole strength into the work,
and was often carried by his natural impetuosity
beyond the bounds both of prudence and of tact.
And besides this flaw in his method of proceed-
ing, he favoured Latin instrumentality exclusively.
His education was no doubt accountable for his
strong aversion to the Slavonic Liturgy, which gave
rise to violent disputes and insurmountable difficulties. At length he threw up the work in despair,
and fled for rest to the peaceful precincts of a con-
vent. Hither, however, in A.D. 994, a summons from
the Roman synod followed him. He was commanded
to return to his post. The order was obeyed, but his
second attempt was as unsuccessful as the first. When

two or three years had expired, he started, commissioned by Gregory V., for Prussia, as a regionary archbishop.

In Bohemia, Adelbert was succeeded by Severus, who accomplished much. But he also was unfriendly to the Slavonic language, and discouraged its use to such an extent, that its liturgy was at last regarded as a sign of heresy. In the year A.D. 1080, duke Ratislav attempted to win from Gregory VII. his approval of the Slavonic service-book used in the abbey of Sazawa. But the pope refused point-blank. " The use of the vernacular," he said, " had been conceded only on account of temporary circumstances, which had now long passed away. As to a vernacular edition of the Scriptures, that was impossible ; it was not the Will of God that the Sacred Word should be everywhere displayed, lest it should be held in contempt, and give rise to error." [1] Twenty years before, indeed, the Synod of Salona had pronounced Methodius a heretic, and the Slavonic alphabet a diabolical invention.

A corner of this chapter must be spared for a few words about *Servia*. This country was peopled by Slavonians, about the time when the emperor Heraclius, perhaps making a virtue of necessity, encouraged a division of the Croats to settle " in Dalmatia, among the Istrian mountains, and on the coast of the Adriatic Gulf." The Servian colonists, called, by themselves, *Srp*, and by the Greeks, *Serbes*, inhabited Upper Mœsia, Dardania, and Dacia, by the invitation of Heraclius, who has thus been said to have assigned

---

[1] See Robertson, iv. 86.

to them "a function which they may even yet discharge, —that of an outlying, independent outpost against a preponderating Northern power."[1]   While acknowledging the general supremacy of the Greek Empire, the early Servians preserved a degree of independence unusual in subject tribes.   With the imperial consent they were governed by native chiefs, and this arrangement appears to have been successful while it held good.[2]   In the eleventh century, however, the Empire stretched out an appropriating hand, and patronage bade fair to expand into mastery.   Of the struggle for freedom which then ensued it does not concern us to speak here.[3]   It is the Servia of an earlier date with which we have to do.

A few sentences will indeed suffice.   For the story of this country, during the process of emancipation from paganism, is but a repetition of the incidents with which, in neighbouring states, we have already become familiar.   Ramifications of the work of Cyril and Methodius extended into Servia.   The Slavonic alphabet made way there, as in Bohemia and Moravia, for Christianity.   The Servians " enjoyed the advantage of a liturgy which was intelligible to them ; and we

---

[1] 'Nationalities,' p, 227.

[2] " The patriarch of Constantinople granted them the privilege of always electing their archbishop from their own national clergy."—Hardwick, p. 136.

[3] When, in A.D. 827, the Byzantine yoke was temporarily shaken off, such allegiance to Christianity as the Servian relations to Constantinople had superinduced seems also to have been repudiated.

find that, early in the 10th century, a considerable
number of Slavonian priests from all the dioceses were
ordained by the bishop of Nona, who was himself a
Slavonian by descent." [1]

That the way of the Cross was here, as always, un-
even and difficult, is not to be doubted. The Ark of
God, guided by a cloud in the day, and by a fiery pillar
in the night, must needs, indeed, go forward until the
Better Land breaks in glory upon us all. But the protecting agencies have often been—still often are—invisible. The cloud over the Tabernacle rests in many
and many a "wilderness of Paran,"—the stepping-
stones in Jordan are often hard to find. The missionary history of Servia was no exception to the
general rule.

It has been noted that—at least in her modern garb
—this country is in one respect "like England."
True, it is a humble possession that, as we learn from
travellers, Servia shares with us.   Only *the flowers*
which we call "common," so dear to us from childhood,— primroses, daisies, violets, forget-me-nots,
honeysuckles, lilacs, and laburnums. These fringe
her lanes, just as they cluster in our own.[2] Yet let
even this trifling characteristic of one of the countries
whose early evangelization we are trying to realize,
be remarked. The Greatest of all Apostles and
Missionaries turned and pointed to the wild flowers
by the wayside, as distinct helps on the heavenward

---

[1] Ranke's ' History of Servia,' p. 4.
[2] ' Servia and the Servians,' Rev. W. Denton, p. 5.

road.[1] "Consider the lilies, how they grow ! they toil not, they spin not ! If then, God so clothe the grass, *how much more you*, O ye of little faith ? "

[1] On the influence of flowers on human life and thought Prof. Ruskin loves to dwell. "The unspeakable azure light along the ground, of the wood-hyacinth in English spring ; the grape-hyacinth, which is in south France, as if a cluster of grapes and a hive of honey had been distilled and compressed together into one small boss of celled and beaded blue ; the lilies of the valley everywhere, in each sweet and wild recess of rocky lands ;—count the influences of these on childish and innocent life ; then measure the mythic power of the hyacinth and asphodel as connected with Greek thoughts of immortality ; finally, take their useful and nourishing power in ancient and modern peasant life, and it will be strange if you do not feel what fixed relation exists between the agencies of the creating spirit in these, and in us who live by them. It is impossible to bring into any tenable compass for our present purpose, even hints of the human influence of the two remaining orders of Amaryllids and Irids ;—only note this generally, that while these, in northern countries, share with the Primulas the fields of spring, it seems that in Greece, the Primulaceæ are not an extended tribe, while the crocus, narcissus, and Amaryllis lutea, the 'lily of the field' (I suspect also that the flower whose name we translate 'violet' was in truth an Iris), represented to the Greek the first coming of the breath of life on the renewed herbage ; and became in his thoughts the true embroidery of the saffron robe of Athena. Later in the year, the dianthus (which, though belonging to an entirely different race of plants, has yet a strange look of having been made out of the grasses by turning the sheaf-membrane at the root of their leaves into a flower) seems to scatter, in multitudinous families, its crimson stars far and wide. But the golden lily and crocus, together with the asphodel, retain always the old Greek's fondest thoughts,—they are only 'golden' flowers that are to burn on the trees and float on the streams of paradise."—'The Queen of the Air,' pp. 98, 99, 100. Cf. also, on passive influences, p. 16, and the remarks on geographical configuration subsequently quoted.

CHAPTER V.

THE CONVERSION OF RUSSIA.

THE territory now known as European Russia, or, at all events, the central and major part of it, seems to have been peopled in the earliest historical times by the Slavonic and Finno-Tartar tribes, of which its present population chiefly consists. But the Slavonic element was not predominant then as it is now, and the *Russian* state, "the first nucleus of that mighty Empire which has united all these various races into one political body," owed its actual foundation to none of them. In the year A.D. 862, according to Nestor, certain tribes, or clans, inhabiting this country, the *Chud*,[1] the *Slavonians*, the *Meria*, the *Krivichi*, and the *Ves*, uprose in arms against the *Varangians*, who three years previously had "come from beyond the sea," demanding tribute. They now "drove the Varangians over the sea, and paid them no tribute; and they began to govern themselves, and there was no justice among them, and clan rose against clan, and there was internal strife between them, and they began to make war upon each other. And they said to each other: 'Let us seek for a prince who can reign over us, and judge what is right.' And they went over the sea

---

[1] "*Tschud*" is one of the names still borne by the Fins.

to the Varangians, to *Rus*, for so were these Varangians called: they were called *Rus*, as others are called *Svie*, others *Nurmane*, others *Angliane*, others *Gote*. The Chud, the Slavonians, the Krivichi, and the Ves said to Rus : 'Our land is large and rich, but there is no order in it; Come ye, and rule and reign over us. And three brothers were chosen, with their whole clan, and they took with them all the Rus, and they came. And the eldest, Rurik, settled in Novgorod.'" The commonly received opinion that these *Rus* were Scandinavians, and probably Swedes, is disputed by many. The dissentients, as is well known, contend that the Russians were, from the very beginning, of purely Slavonic extraction. Into the general merits of this question we cannot here enter, but must restrict ourselves to a few remarks on the word which has provoked so much and such animated discussion.

To the Greeks the *Rus* were known before the middle of the 9th century. By them they were called *Rhôs* ['Ρως]; and, about a century later, *Rusioi* ['Ρούσιοι]. The meaning of the name *Rhôs*, however, in Dr. Latham's opinion, on the other hand, is "ambiguous, up to the middle of the 10th century."[1] Be that as it may, a Greek author, Theophanes Isaakios, in describing an attack on the Danubian Bulgarians by Constantine Copronymus, in the year A.D. 773, employs the expression *rusioi* in a manner which casts some little light on the subject, even if it be only negative. He records that Constantine

---

[1] 'Russian and Turk,' p. 375.

followed his army on board certain vessels which he
describes as τὰ ῥούσια χελάνδια. By believers in
the Slavonic origin of the Russ, these words have been
translated, *the Russian galleys*. But it is pointed out
by Dr. Vilhelm Thomsen that before the 10th century
the Greeks always spoke of the *Rus* as *Rhôs* ['Ρῶς],
and that the adjective formed from that word was
ῥωσικός. He therefore infers that only the common
signification, *red*, is to be assigned on this occasion
to the Greek word ῥούσιος. It is known that the
ships which conveyed the emperor with his guard
and attendants, were painted red, and Dr. Thomsen
accordingly translates τὰ ῥούσια χελάνδια into "the
red, or imperial galleys," as distinct from the common
war, or transport galleys, in which the army sailed.[1]
He also considers it worthy of remark, that " the Russ
did not use ' chelandia,' which were a very large kind
of ship, but they always used small ships, or boats." [2]

" The first time the Greeks came in contact with
the Russ," he continues, "as far as we know, was in
A.D. 838 or 839, and this is also the only time the
name ' Russ '[3] is mentioned in any document before
the time of Rurik." [4]

Before quitting the subject, a slight reference may
be made to one division of the interesting evidence

[1] 'Origin of the Ancient Russ,' p. 22.
[2] "The invaders from territories afterwards Russian," writes
Dr. Latham, "descend upon the Greeks of Macedonia in
boats made out of a single tree [*monoxyla,*] which implies the
navigation of a river."—'Russian and Turk,' p. 374.
[3] 'Ρῶς.
[4] 'Origin of the Ancient Russ,' p. 22.

furnished by the same writer in proof of the Scandinavian origin of the ancient *Russ* clan. The emperor Constantine Porphyrogenitus, in describing the rapids of the Dnieper, enumerates the cataracts in both their Slavonic and their Russ names, at the same time explaining the meaning of the words. Dr. Thomsen shows that the Slavonic appellations are "really pure Slavonic, and some of them completely agree with the modern Russian names of the rapids," while the names called *Russ* by Constantine are found to be Scandinavian, or Old Norse words. But the pages devoted to this examination by the author of the 'Origin of the Ancient Russ,' should be read as they stand. They undeniably lend a valuable support to the view that the *Rus̓* were of Swedish derivation. The eastward stream of Scandinavian colonization set out from the shores of Sweden, and the name Rus' or Rhôs ['Ρως] seems to have been of Eastern coinage, rather than the patronymic of the clan in use among themselves.

In the year A.D. 865, the Russ sailed down the Dnieper, crossed the Black Sea, and after plundering its islands and coasts, and spreading general consternation around them, made their appearance under the walls of Constantinople. If we follow Nestor's chronology, Rurik had barely settled himself and his people in their new quarters, before their longing eyes were cast on the wealthy Oriental capital.

The inhabitants of Constantinople seem to have been too completely paralyzed by terror to attempt any systematic defence. They implored the Virgin to come to their aid, accompanying their invocations by ceremonies of a conciliatory character. These solemnities were conducted by the patriarch Photius, two sermons by whom, delivered "on the occasion of the attack of the Rhôs," were discovered in Russia not many years ago.

Legend asserts that a miracle rewarded the faith of the Greeks. A violent storm arose, and wrought such havoc among the vessels of the "Rhôs" that very few escaped demolition. We have the testimony of tradition, that so deeply were the barbarian invaders impressed by this manifestation of Divine power, that they forthwith became believers in the God Who had confounded their plans. "They were," asserts M. Mouravieff, "the firstfruits of their people to the Lord. The hymn of victory of the Greek Church, 'To the protecting conductress,' in honour of the most holy Virgin, has remained a memorial of this triumph, and even now, among ourselves, concludes the Office for the First Hour in the daily Matins, for that was indeed the first hour of salvation to the land of Russia."[1] Photius also, in an encyclical letter, A.D. 866, to the Oriental bishops, ascribes to the Greek Church the honour of the conversion of the audacious *Rhôs*, that is, of those representatives of the general body who had prepared to assail Constantinople. But whether a single "grain of mustard-seed" was or was not carried home by the invaders, it seems clear that the general conversion mentioned by

---

[1] 'History of the Church of Russia,' p. 8.

Photius was neither real nor lasting. For in spite of a struggling ray of light here and there, paganism was all but universal in Russia for nearly a hundred years afterwards.

In the year A.D. 907, as Nestor relates, the Russ reappeared in the immediate neighbourhood of Constantinople. This time, however, the Greeks had effectually barred the sea approach. But Oleg, the commander of the expedition, was nothing daunted. We read that he caused his ships[1] to be dragged ashore, and mounted on wheels. In this novel position the wind filled their sails, and the Greeks were appalled by the unnatural apparition of a hostile fleet sailing towards the city on dry land ! The story ends with the abject humiliation of the besieged, who offered the ingenious Oleg any amount of tribute if he would but make peace with them. That he dictated terms highly advantageous to himself we need not to be assured.

Other expeditions followed, which it is not our province to recount, but we may observe that their object was sometimes rather commercial than warlike. In their readiness to adapt themselves either to trade or war, the ancient Russ strongly remind us of the Norse Viking, of whose kin they are supposed to have been. A quaint picture of them survives, drawn by an Arabian hand. Though due allowance must be made for probable high colouring, the sketch

---

[1] The small size of the Russ ships has already been noted. See p. 76.

is too graphic to be altogether omitted. "I saw
the Russ," says Ibn Fadhlan, ambassador among
the Bulgarians, in A.D. 921 and 922,—"I saw the
Russ, who had arrived with their wares, and had
encamped upon the river Itil [Volga]. Never saw
I people of more perfect stature ; they are tall like
palm-trees, ruddy and fair-haired. They clothe themselves neither in jackets nor in kaftans, but the men
wear a coarse cloak, which they throw over the one
side, so that one of their hands is left free. Every
man carries an axe, a knife, and a sword. Without
these weapons they are never seen. The women
wear on the bosom a small capsule of iron, copper,
silver, or gold, according to the wealth and standing
of the husband. On the capsule is a ring, and on
that a knife, fastened equally on the bosom. When
a man possesses 10,000 dirhems [silver coins], he has
a chain made for his wife ; if he has 20,000, she gets
two neckchains," and so on. Their greatest ornament consists of green glass beads. They are very
fond of them, and will pay a dirhem apiece for them,
and string them as neckchains for their wives." Ibn
Fadhlan goes on to describe the devotions of a Russ
merchant-warrior on his arrival on strange shores.
Leaving a present of eatables before the wooden image
which he sets up, he says, "I pray thee to grant me
a purchaser well-provided with gold and silver coins,
who will buy all *as I wish, without bargaining.*" If
prosperous business follows this petition, he testifies
his gratitude by a sacrifice of sheep and oxen.
Another Oriental writer records of the early Russ,

that when a son is born to any of them, the father
throws a sword at him, saying : " I do not leave thee
any property ; thine is only what thou gainest with
thy sword." [1]

But it is time to turn to the religious aspect, in
which Russia and the Russians chiefly concern us
here.   And first, we are confronted by legends.
" There is one feature of Russian scenery truly grand ;
its network of magnificent rivers."   This is the observation of the author of the well-known ' Lectures
on the Eastern Church.'   "These," he continues,
" important for its political and commercial interests,
are the threads with which the country's religious
destinies have been always curiously interwoven.
Turn your mind's eye to the vast stream of the
Dnieper, the old Borysthenes, as it rolls into the
Euxine !   Over the banks of that stream, 500 miles
from its mouth, hangs a low range of hills,—low for
any other country, but high for the level steppes of
Russia, and therefore called *Kieff*, ' the mountain.'
From that mountain, we are told, a noble prospect
commands the course of the river ; and up the course
of that river, on his way from Sinope to Rome, came,
according to the ancient legend, Andrew, the Apostle
of Greece, the Apostle of Scythia ; and as he rose in
the morning, and saw the heights of Kieff, on which
he planted the first Cross, he said : ' See you those
hills ?   For on those hills shall hereafter shine forth

[1] Dr. Vilhelm Thomsen, ' Origin of the Russ,' &c., pp. 30,
32, 33.

the Grace of God. There shall be a great city, and God shall cause many churches to rise within it.' "[1] Another legend, still more fabulous in its groundwork, connects the entrance of Christianity into Russia with the flowing current of a river. A saint, so shadowy that his name is scarcely known, cast ignominiously into the Tiber for his faith's sake, floated miraculously from the Mediterranean to the Atlantic, and from the Baltic into the river Neva. On the bosom of its placid waters the Neva bore him into Lake Ladoga. Thence he passed by successive stages up to the walls of Novgorod.

" The Dnieper and the Neva are the two inlets by which life and light have penetrated into the vast deserts of Russia, from the East and from the West."[2] Calling to mind the soothing effect of the various broad, majestic rivers, as we watched them breaking the monotony of the silent plains, in our survey of the Slavonic countries, before closing the first chapter of this volume, the religious myths of the Dnieper and the Neva commend themselves, in spite of their fancifulness, to our affections. Nor can we forget—once more to glance at the old word *Russ*—that the signification of the Scandinavian synonym for it is *rower, boatman,* or *fisher.*[3] But the enchanted land of legend must no longer detain us ; we are stepping now across its border into the

---

[1] ' Eastern Church,' pp. 292, 293.

[2] ' Ibid., p. 293.

[3] Dr. V. Thomsen, p. 96. See also the note.

domain of history.   Simultaneously, let us exchange
the old-world form, *Russ*, for the modern *Russians*.
" It was once," says Dr. Thomsen, " the ancient
Slavonic appellation of the Northmen, and has at
last come to signify a purely Slavonic nationality."

In the middle of the 10th century, the widowed
princess Olga, lately released from the cares of
regency, travelled from Kief to Constantinople.
Whether her visit had political objects, or whether
she was prompted to pay it solely, as some say, by a
desire to know more of the holy faith of which only
glimpses had been vouchsafed her at home, cannot
be positively decided.   But her sojourn in the
imperial city was a turning-point in her career.
Baptism was administered to her by the patriarch
Polyeuctes, the emperor Constantine Porphyrogenitus
officiating as sponsor.   Polyeuctes then solemnly
addressed the princess, predicting that through her
instrumentality Russia should be richly blessed.
" Olga," writes M. Mouravieff, " now become *Helena*
by baptism, that she might resemble both in name
and deed the mother of Constantine the Great,
stood meekly bowing down her head, and drinking
in, as a sponge that is thirsty of moisture, the
instructions of the prelate." [1]   His injunctions, which
were plentiful, she is recorded to have " observed
with holy exactness on her return to her own
country."

This pious princess strove, by all the means in her

[1] ' Russian Church,' p. 9.

power, to induce her son, Sviatoslav, to accept the creed which she had speedily learnt to hold dear. But on him her efforts were quite thrown away. He heeded his mother's entreaties only so far as to abstain from persecuting those of his subjects who, moved by her example, had embraced Christianity. For himself, absorbed as he was in perpetual military expeditions, he was a soldier cast on the roughest scale. Inured to the hardships inseparable from his mode of life, impervious to danger, indifferent to luxury, he neither knew nor cared about a higher standard than that of his forefathers. The ground was his accustomed bed, a saddle his pillow; his diet coarse and spare. He died, A.D. 972, in battle. His foes, the Pechenegians, are said to have fashioned his skull into a drinking-cup, inscribing it with these elegiac words : "In seeking for that which belonged to others, he lost his own." [1]

During his continually recurring absences from home, Sviatoslav had been accustomed to confide his children to his mother's care. That princess naturally sought to win their childish hearts to the gentle influences of the Gospel. Some latent impressions favourable to Christianity her youngest grandson, Vladimir,[2] doubtless owed to her. Nevertheless when, on the death of his brother Yarapolk, for which indeed he was held responsible, he mounted the throne, no signs of a gracious character revealed themselves.

[1] Mouravieff, p. 352 [notes].
[2] Sometimes called Valdemar, as by the Norwegians. See 'The Conversion of the Northmen,' p. 80.

He was, on the contrary, a bitter and bigoted pagan.
He increased the number of heathen altars and idols,
and in his zeal for sacrificial offerings to Perun, did
not scruple to look around for human victims.   Two
Christians, by name Theodore and John, suffered
death at the hands of an infuriated populace,
because one of them recoiled from the royal demand
for his son as a pagan sacrifice.   " The contrast
between the cruelty and vices of Vladimir when a
heathen, and the mildness of his disposition and the
purity of his morals after his conversion, are adduced
by the annalists, as strong proofs of the Divine character of the religion he had embraced." [1]

It seems to have occurred to many missionaries of
varying types, that a chief of such mark should not
be left at the mercy of his own violent passions.
The spiritual well-being of Vladimir accordingly
became the object of laborious journeys, of much
exertion, and of redundant eloquence. Guidance was
first volunteered by the Bulgarian Mussulmans from
the Volga.   "Believe, O prince," said they, "in our
religion ! and honour Mahomet."

"But what," asked Vladimir, "may your religion
be ? "   The servants of the Prophet described some
of the leading advantages and prohibitions of their
faith.   " Drink no wine ! " cried Vladimir, echoing
one peculiarly distasteful injunction which had caught
his ear ; "drinking is the great delight of the Russians ;
we cannot live without it ! " This clearly was not

---

[1] Mouravieff, p. 360.

the religion for him, and its apologists retreated, crest-
fallen.

The attention of the king was now solicited by a
deputation from the Chazarian Jews, who boasted of
the ancient glories of Jerusalem, and the privileges of
her children. But the astute Vladimir inquired where
their country lay, upon which they were fain to confess that they were suffering for the misdoings of their
ancestors, and were scattered abroad by a justly dis-
pleased God. With a contemptuous intimation that
their fate was but a poor inducement to others to
worship their God, Vladimir, a firm believer in " the
Divine right of success," dismissed the Jewish envoys.

And now arrived delegates from Western Christendom. They quoted the pope as their authority.
" Ours," they urged, " is the right religion. We fear
God, Who made the heaven and earth, the stars and
the moon, and every living creature, whilst thy gods
are of wood."

But Vladimir rejected their appeal. His ancestors,
he said, knew nothing about the pope. So the learned
doctors retired, having, like their predecessors, accomplished nothing.

Last of all came a Greek emissary. He was
neither "a priest nor a missionary, but a philosopher." [1] He disclosed to Vladimir the " abominable
practices" of the Mahometans who had urged their
religion upon him, and confirmed the disgust already
conceived for them by the king. He expounded

[1] Stanley's ' Eastern Church,' p. 298.

some of the errors of the Latin Church, whose representatives had also ineffectually recommended their
creed to the fastidious Vladimir. "They," observed
the 'philosopher,' "celebrate the mass with unleavened
bread ; therefore they have not the true religion."
" But Jews have been here," said the prince, "who told
me that both the Germans and Greeks believe on One
Whom they crucified !" "That is even so," replied
the learned Greek. "But *why*," urged Vladimir, "*why
was He crucified ?*" Then the philosopher, secure
of his listener's patient attention, recited the Sacred
Story from beginning to end. The curiosity of the
king was plainly awakened, but the Greek, perceiving
the drift of the man's character, did not trust alone
to the beseeching force of pathos. He concluded by
bringing the element of fear also into play. Producing a painted picture of the Last Judgment, he
laid it before Vladimir. Like Bogoris, the wild
Russian chief was greatly moved. The philosopher
pointed to the throng of the blessed, joyfully entering
the kingdom prepared for them from the foundation
of the world, and contrasted their condition with the
terror of the groups on the left hand. In baptism,
he said, his royal host would find both the entrance
to bliss, and the escape from woe.

But Vladimir, though he " heard him gladly," and
though he was " burdened with the heavy sins of a
tumultuous youth," shrank from committing himself
to a course which he had not thoroughly weighed. He
therefore postponed a decision, but the philosopher
withdrew loaded with marks of his favour.

The following year the king laid before the elders of his council the rival pleas of these variously recommended forms of faith, and solicited their advice. The nobles mused awhile, and then counselled their master to ascertain how each religion worked at home. This, they thought, would be more practical evidence than the plausible representations of professors. On this suggestion Vladimir acted. Envoys were chosen, —presumably, for their powers of observation,—and the embassy of inquiry started.

"This public agreement," says the historian of the Russian Church, "explains in some degree the sudden and general acceptance of Christianity which shortly after followed in Russia. It is probable that not only the chiefs, but the common people also, were expecting and ready for the change."[1] A report, far from encouraging, was in due time received from the ambassadors. Of the German and Roman, as well as the Jewish, religions in daily life, they spoke in very disparaging terms, while they declared the Mussulman creed, when reduced to practice, to be utterly out of the question. Disappointed in all these quarters, they now proceeded, by command, to Constantinople, or, as the Russians called it, *Tzaragorod.*

Basil Porphyrogenitus, who at the time, A.D. 987, shared the Byzantine throne with his brother Constantine, was keenly alive to the possible political results of the formal visit. He directed the patriarch

---

[1] Mouravieff, p. 12.

to gratify the strangers at the outset, with an imposing display of ritual. "Let them see," said he, "the glory of our God."

Singularly enough, the Russian envoys, accustomed, as we must suppose them to have been, only to the barest simplicity of life, had complained not only of the paucity of decoration in the Latin churches, but of a lack of beauty in their appointments. Thus the preparations of the patriarch were accurately fitted to their expectant frame of mind.

They were led into the church of S. Sophia, gleaming with variegated marbles, and porphyries, and jasper, at that time "the masterpiece of Christian architecture."[1] The building glittered with gold and rich mosaics. The service was that of a high festival, either of St. John Chrysostom, or of the Death of the Virgin,[2] and was conducted by the patriarch in person, clad in his most gorgeous vestments. Tapers blazed, anthems pealed, fragrant clouds of incense floated upward. Melodious and rhythmic chanting broke softly on the ear. The brilliant scene appealed vehemently to every sense, and produced an effect on the dazzled Russians which surpassed the most sanguine calculations of the emperor.

While they gazed in rapturous wonder on the superb spectacle, their critical perceptions became, not unnaturally, somewhat confused. When the deacons and sub-deacons poured forth in procession from the sanctuary, wings of white linen adorning their

[1] 'Eastern Church,' p. 300.   [2] Ibid.

shoulders, and torches flashing in their hands, and the people fell on their knees, crying "Kyrie Eleison!" the envoys, completely carried away by emotion, seized their guides by the hand. All that they had previously seen, they said, had in truth been magnificent and solemn, but now they had beheld the supernatural. Angels, in lustrous apparel, and chanting in the air, "Holy! Holy! Holy!" took part, they perceived, in the services of this Church. "We want no further proof," cried they; "send us home again!"

On their return to Vladimir, they dilated with eager delight on the wonders they had seen. The king listened gravely to their glowing account of "the temple, like which there was none upon earth." After sweetness, they protested, bitterness would be unbearable, so that—whatever others might do—they at all events should at once abandon heathenism.

While the king hesitated, his boyars[1] turned the scale by reminding him that if the creed of the Greeks had not indeed had much to recommend it, his pious and sagacious grandmother, princess Olga, would not have loved and obeyed it. Her name acted like a talisman. Vladimir resolved to conform to Christianity. But still, fondly clinging to the habits of his

[1] "The boyars were nobles of the first class. In peace they were governors of towns and districts, in which they administered justice; also they attended the court, and formed the privy council of the sovereign. In war, they led their retainers to the field, and exercised nearly the same authority over them that the feudal nobility of France and England did over their vassals."—Mouravieff, p. 354.

orefathers, he cherished the idea of wooing and winning his new religion by the sword.

He determined that the people whose faith he intended ultimately to accept should witness some display of his power. In execution of this purpose, he besieged the city of Cherson, in the Crimea, and vowed that if his attempt succeeded, he would forthwith be baptized. The city, which acknowledged the imperial sway, long resisted the Russian attack. At last, however, intelligence was craftily conveyed to Vladimir, by means of an arrow shot from the town, that his success might be ensured by cutting off the water-supply from the aqueducts.

Acting on this hint, he speedily mastered the place. His next step was to require of the emperor Basil the hand of his sister Anne in marriage, nor did he scruple to threaten that in the event of refusal he would deal with Constantinople as he had dealt with Cherson. Maintaining the dignity of the purple in the face of danger, Basil replied that the proposal could only be entertained on one condition. Vladimir must adopt Christianity. To this counter-proposition the Russian prince, already pledged to baptism by his vow, consented. It now only remained, therefore, to reconcile the princess Anne to her fate, from which she might excusably recoil. But in consideration of the glory to be won for the Church, and the peril to be averted from the State, she agreed to fulfil the engagement contracted for her by her brother. Attended by an escort of clergy, she sailed for Cherson, and her arrival was signalized by the baptism of Vladimir. He is said to have been suffering at the time from some malady affecting his eyesight. No sooner, however, according to this account, had he emerged from the waters of baptism, than he found that he was healed. "Now," exclaimed the royal neophyte, "I have seen the true God!"

Many of Vladimir's courtiers, influenced by his example, received Christianity; and having built a church at Cherson, and restored the city to the emperors, he started homewards, accompanied by his bride and her bevy of ecclesiastics. Arrived at Kief, the king peremptorily prescribed baptism to his twelve sons, and applied himself, with characteristic vigour, to abolish all outward tokens of heathenism.

The colossal wooden idol, Perun, was dragged ignominiously across the hills at a horse's tail, flogged the while by a dozen mounted attendants. Finally, the degraded image was flung scornfully into the Dnieper. The people, beholding with dismay the lamentable plight of their venerated deity, followed it for some little distance along the river-banks, adjuring it to assert its power. But as the helplessness of Perun under these adverse circumstances gradually manifested itself, the chase was abandoned, and the god disappeared in the rush of the "rapids."

And now the waters of the Dnieper, which had remorselessly swallowed the deposed idol, were devoted to a very different purpose.

A royal proclamation was issued, that "whoever, on the morrow, should not repair to the river, whether rich or poor," should be held as the king's enemy.

"The morrow," accordingly, witnessed a remarkable scene. The people of Kief obediently crowded to the river-side, and there, as one flock, were baptized. "Some," says Nestor, "stood in the water up to their necks; others, up to their breasts, holding their young children in their arms," while priests, stationed on the banks, read the baptismal service.

The joy of the king, who for some time watched the affecting scene in silence, knew no bounds. Words at last broke from his lips, addressed to Him in Whose rule and governance are the hearts of kings.

Let us listen to the Prayer of Vladimir. "O great God! Who hast made heaven and earth, look down upon these Thy new people! Grant them, O Lord, to know Thee, the true God, as Thou hast been made known to Christian lands; and confirm in them a true and unfailing faith. And assist me, O Lord, against my enemy that opposes me; that, trusting in Thee, and in Thy power, I may overcome all his wiles!" [1]

Under the auspices of the sovereign, the stately church of St. Basil soon arose, on the very spot recently occupied by the temple of Perun.

Kief became the centre of Christian influence, whence evangelizing energies radiated in all directions.

Schools and churches were built, while Michael, the first metropolitan, attended by his bishops, "made progresses into the interior of Russia, everywhere baptizing and instructing the people." The Greek

---

[1] Mouravieff, p. 15.

canon law came into force, and the use of the service-
book and choral music of the Greek communion
became general, while, in the Slavonic Scriptures and
Liturgy of Cyril and Methodius, a road was discovered
which led straight to the hearts of the native population. "Cyril and Methodius, if any one, must be
considered by anticipation as the first Christian
teachers of Russia ; their rude alphabet first instructed
the Russian nation in letters, and, by its quaint Greek
characters, still testifies in every Russian book, and
on every Russian house or shop, the Greek source of
the religion and literature of the empire."[1] A year
after his conversion, Vladimir summoned builders from
Greece, and laid at Kief the foundation-stone of the
first cathedral built of stone in Russia. This church
was intended by him as a memorial of his baptism.
"Thus," says the Russian Chronicle, "did Christianity
diffuse her light over Russia, like the rising sun, with
progressively increasing splendour, and Vladimir rejoiced thereat, and was liberal towards the poor and
afflicted, and distributed his gifts among all the people."
Under Leontius, the second metropolitan, the dioceses
of Novgorod, Rostoff, Chernigoff, Vladimir, and Bel-
gorod, were created. Joachim, bishop of Novgorod,
waged war against the idols as heartily as the king
himself. The image of Perun, in his city, was
handled as roughly as its namesake at Kief had
been. Pagan altars were destroyed, if not with the
open concurrence of the people, at least without oppo-

---

[1] 'Eastern Church,' pp. 310, 311.

sition. Along the track of commerce and civilization, the missionary work progressed with comparative ease. But in less-favoured districts the idols were only displaced with the greatest difficulty. In the Rostoff diocese, for instance, the two first bishops, Theodore and Hilarion, were forcibly expelled, and Christianity was obliged for many years to contest every step of its onward and upward way.

Twenty-seven years after his conversion, Vladimir, the royal apostle[1] of Russia, died: A.D. 1015. A guardian saint of his country he became as a matter of course. His body was laid in a marble coffin, and buried by John, the third metropolitan, in the church of the Tithes, at Kief, near the tomb of Anne, his Greek queen. The remains of his revered grandmother, Olga, were removed to the same spot. " The union of Vladimir with Anne," it has been emphatically declared, "is still a living power. The Church of Russia cannot be divided from the general fortunes of Oriental Christendom."[2]

---

[1] " There is no apostle of Russia except Vladimir, who bears the same title as that of Constantine, ' Isapostolos ;' '*Vladimir equal to an Apostle.*' "—Stanley's ' Eastern Church,' p. 307.

[2] Ibid., p. 304.

CHAPTER VI.

"THE chief fact in the ethnology of the Poles," writes Dr. Latham, "is its extreme character; inasmuch as either they or the Bohemians are the types of the Western, as opposed to the Eastern, Slavonians. Like that of the Servians, their blood is comparatively pure and unmixed, at least in the western parts of the area. Like the Carinthians, Carniolans, Styrians, and Slovaks, their line of ethnological and historical influences has run from west to east, being—politically and ecclesiastically—German and Roman, rather than Turk or Greek."[1]

It seems probable that Poland was not wholly unaffected by the labours of Cyril and Methodius. Some echoes of the teaching of those devoted missionaries no doubt found their way from Moravia into that country. And when Christian refugees, flying from the horrors of the Hungarian invasion, passed through Poland, their witness must have confirmed the vague rumours of good tidings already heard. Some attempts were made to introduce the Slavonic Liturgy, and to persuade the people in dif-

---

[1] 'Native Races,' p. 255. The word *Pole* means "a dweller in a flat country."

ferent parts of the country to lay aside their old faith
in favour of the new.   But no tangible results sprang
from these disjointed and desultory efforts.   Christianity remained, practically, a dead letter as far as
Poland was concerned, until the year A.D. 965, when
a marriage occurred which speedily wrought mighty
changes there.

Duke Mieceslav I. married Dambrowka, daughter
of the Bohemian prince Boleslav the Cruel, and was
induced by his bride to be baptized, and to accept
the faith which she professed.

The proclivities of Mieceslav, who acknowledged
the German Empire, and was a member of its diets,
could not but tinge the line of belief prescribed by
him to his subjects.   His preferences being all anti-
Slavonic, the Eastern characteristics of the early and
fragmentary creed imported from Moravia found no
favour in his eyes.   Nor was he content with a
passive disapproval.   He proceeded to enforce that
form of Christianity which he discerned to be politically advantageous to himself.   Coercion was the
only method that he recognized.

Christianity was to be the national religion, and
any evasion of this command would henceforth be
punished by the severest penalties.   Such were the
proclamations which greeted the astonished ears of
his people.   An instance of the duke's rigorous policy
may be adduced, in an enactment declaring that any
infringement of an order which prohibited the eating
of meat between Septuagesima and Easter, should be
followed by the loss of the offender's teeth.   But that

such extreme measures did not strike the ecclesiastics of early days in the light wherein we regard them, we learn from the comments of Dietmar, bishop of Merseburg, upon this very edict. He argues, in vindication of the duke's sternness, that none but the roughest modes of treatment were suitable to people who were only comparable to cattle. What they were too stubborn to accept graciously, and too dull to perceive spontaneously, must, it was clear, be beaten into them. The Poles, however, were not disposed quietly to accept the castigation considered so wholesome by the bishop. They vehemently resented the severity of Mieceslav, and lost no opportunity of thwarting and opposing him. Thus, as might be expected, Christianity made very little way.

The Polish bishopric of Posen owed its creation to the emperor Otho I., who established it five years after the marriage of Mieceslav with Dambrowka. It was subject, in the first instance, to the archiepiscopal see of Mayence, but was subsequently transferred to the jurisdiction of the archbishop of Magdeburg.[1] The Latin predilections of Mieceslav, already strong, were strengthened tenfold by his marriage to a fourth wife, Oda, daughter of a German marquis. She had been a nun, but the violation of her vows which marriage involved was condoned by the clergy, in consideration of her activity in all charitable and religious works. Under her auspices

---

[1] Krasinski's 'Reformation in Poland,' i. p. 26.

large bodies of ecclesiastics trooped into Poland, from France, Italy, and Germany. Beneath the weight of the Latin usages, now everywhere in vogue, the Byzantine forms soon sank, completely overwhelmed. Poland was a child of the Western Church.

About the year A.D. 1000, the emperor Otho III. undertook a pilgrimage to the shrine of St. Adelbert, at Gnesen, the Polish capital, and was received by Boleslav, the son and successor of Mieceslav, with becoming pomp and splendour.

That there was a political side to this devotional expedition, there can be little doubt. Before the visit came to an end, Boleslav received the title of king, while Gnesen was elevated to the rank of a metropolitan see, and to its control were referred the dioceses of Breslau and Cracow, as well as Colberg in East Pomerania. "The popes," says Mr. Robertson, "were careful to draw close the bonds which connected Poland with Rome, and from an early time a yearly tribute of a penny was paid by every Pole, with the exception of the clergy and the nobles, to the treasury of St. Peter."[1] This custom is dated by some from the imperial visit to Gnesen just described, while others believe it to have an earlier origin.

King Boleslav pursued his father's relentless policy. The vernacular was the object of his unwearying hatred, and no steps tending to its abolition were left untaken. Paganism, on the other hand, was hunted to the death.

---

[1] 'History of the Christian Church,' p. 88.

Resistance, however, was persistently, though ineffectually, offered, and thus Poland, throughout the life of Boleslav, was the battle-field of the creeds. Nor was the reign of his successor, Mieceslav II., at all more tranquil. His consort, Rixa by name, was a niece of the emperor Otho III., and naturally furthered German interests by all the means in her power.

The tithes exacted by the Latin clergy were an ever fruitful source of discontent, and revolt succeeded revolt until the death of Mieceslav. His son being a minor, Rixa now governed as regent, and her unpopularity increased with her power. At last, the disaffection of the people swelled into such an alarming and threatening clamour, that she was driven to acknowledge that the only prudent course left open to her was flight. She accordingly retreated, with her young son Casimir, into Germany.

And now Poland became the prey of anarchy. The pagans, aware that an opportunity for revenge had occurred, raised their heads with renewed courage. Springing from their cowering attitude of sullen, stifled rage, into a sudden and terrible activity, they hastened to turn the tables upon a persecuting Church. Monasteries and churches were ruthlessly destroyed, the bishops and the clergy were maltreated, banished, and even in some instances murdered, and heathenism triumphed once more.

The ringleader of the pagan insurgents, named Maslav, was acknowledged as the ruler of the Poles; yet no title of honour was accorded to him. He was called neither king, nor prince, nor duke,—he was the mere representative of an infuriated populace, who found, perhaps half-unconsciously, in this fierce explosion of revenge on the faith so lately dominant, an outlet also for the ancient republican instincts of the Slavonians.   In the German ascendency which they loathed, the people saw embodied the monarchical form of government as well as the foreign form of religion.

The struggle was desperate, and continued for years, the pagans contriving, as a rule, to keep the upper hand.   But at last the fury of the combatants began to be spent, and the country yearned for some kind of order, after the long and wild misrule which it had been enduring.   Inquiring eyes were turned in the direction whither Casimir, the heir-apparent, had disappeared.   And finally, it was generally agreed to propose his return.

Casimir, in the mean time, had entered a Benedictine monastery,[1] and had added to the vows of his order the responsibilities of ordination.   Consequently, when his penitent subjects proffered him the Polish crown, they met with an unexpected check in the declaration of the abbot that he could not liberate the royal monk from his obligations, A.D. 1034.   In this difficulty, the interposition of the pope, Benedict IX., was solicited.   After much debating, the pontiff consented to cancel Casimir's

---

[1] Either at Clugny or at Braunweiler.—Hardwick's 'Church History,' p. 126.

vows, and permission was accorded to him both to marry and to accept the crown of Poland.

Casimir accordingly ascended the throne, and under his patronage Christianity once more throve apace. But he testified his gratitude to the pope, to whose dispensation he owed his crown, by un-remitting warfare against such remnants of the Slavonic customs and services as had survived the many persecutions levelled against them. Among all the Slavonic nations, there is not one in which mental cultivation was visibly so little affected by Christianity as Poland.[1] "Upon its language" we are assured, the new faith "exerted no influence at all. The teachers of Christianity in this country were, for nearly five centuries, foreigners; viz. Germans and Italians. Hence arose that unnatural neglect of the vernacular tongue, of which these were ignorant,—the private influence of the German, still visible in the Polish language,—and the unlimited dominion of the Latin. *Slavic*, *Polish*, and *heathenish*, were to them synonymous words."[2]

We have noted that the Pomeranian diocese of Colberg was subjected by Otho III. to the archi-episcopal control of Gnesen. Eastern Pomerania had been conquered by king Boleslav, and incorporated with the Polish territories. The first bishop appointed to the see of Colberg was a German, who accom-plished next to nothing in the interests of Chris-

[1] 'Historical View of the Languages and Literature of the Slavic nations.'—Talvi. Prefaced by Dr. Robinson, p. 224.
[2] Ibid.

tianity, and was eventually murdered, in the year A.D. 1015, while absent on a journey to Russia.

The Pomeranians resented and never ceased to conspire against the dominion of the Poles. Their continually recurring rebellions, however, were invariably unsuccessful, and only provoked their masters into threatening fresh chastisements, which could be averted in one way alone ; viz., by submission, while there was yet time, to baptism. This rite was consequently regarded as a symbol of degradation, and detested accordingly.

In the year A.D. 1121, Western Pomerania was also subdued, and the Polish yoke pressed heavily upon the inhabitants, of whom an oath to adopt Christianity was required. Boleslav III. was merciless in his treatment. He thought to implant Christianity among the Pomeranians by his sword, and massacre after massacre failed to convince him that the weapon was ill suited to its work. An attack was made, in mid-winter, on Stettin, the capital of Pomerania. No quarter was given, and no limits imposed on the barbarity of the besiegers. Three years afterwards, the horrors of that time were mutely attested by heaps of bleaching skeletons. Eighteen thousand Pomeranian soldiers were killed ; while eight thousand, having purchased bare life by renouncing their idols and submitting to baptism, were sent into Poland, and distributed among the frontier garrisons.

Finding that his engines of destruction did not compass his ends, Boleslav, much at a loss for methods, commended the evangelization of Pomerania

to the Polish bishops. But they declined his proposal with precipitation. The year after the reduction
of Western Pomerania, however, a volunteer presented
himself. He was a Spanish ecclesiastic, named
Bernard, who had been raised at Rome to the
episcopal rank. He now declared himself ready to
undertake the mission from which every one else
shrank. Boleslav did not disguise the truth. He
explained that the task would abound with difficulties,
and that the tenacity of the Pomeranians with respect
to their idols was of such a character as to hold out
small hope of a successful issue.

Bernard, however, was nothing daunted. He was,
indeed, ill adapted to the work he courted. A
Spaniard by birth, and ignorant alike of the language
and the tastes of the Pomeranians, he was also an
ascetic, which, to such easy, merry, and careless
people as those whom he proposed to convert, was a
peculiarly incomprehensible phenomenon.

Untroubled, notwithstanding, by any misgivings, he
started on his mission, duly attended by an inter-
preter supplied by Boleslav, and a chaplain. But his
appearance at Julin, barefooted, and in the attire
of a humble mendicant, was greeted with unsparing
ridicule. The contempt of the astonished Pomeranians was unbounded.

When Bernard solemnly declared that he was God's
messenger, they scornfully retorted that the Lord of
all power and might, Whom he described, was not
likely to send a beggar as His representative. It was
obvious they with one accord declared, that God's

glory was only a convenient cloak assumed to hide the real object of their visitor, which was relief in his poverty-stricken state. Bernard had better retrace his steps as quickly as possible, for they would not tolerate such imposition. But the Spaniard persisted. He was willing, he proudly asserted, to be flung into a blazing fire, to furnish proof of his Divine credentials. If he issued from it unsinged, as other servants of God had been permitted to do before him, he presumed that the haughty Pomeranians would abandon their incredulity. This proposal, however, served only to confirm the impression of his audience that he was insane. Again they bade him begone. But Bernard, in his hasty zeal, struck down one of the native idols, upon which an uproar arose, from which he was only too thankful to escape by sea. The parting taunt which reached his ears was, that his taste for preaching might now be freely indulged. He could address the fish and the sea-birds at his leisure.

Greatly discomfited, he now retreated to Bamberg, where he fell in with the bishop of that see, who immediately struck him as peculiarly fitted for the undertaking which he had himself just relinquished in despair.

Otho, bishop of Bamberg, was a Suabian of high birth. His education had been liberal, and he had lived in Poland in the capacity of chaplain to duke Ratislav.[1]

As the successful conductor of several negotiations

---

[1] Or Radislav.

at the German court, he had rendered many services to his patron, whose marriage with a daughter of the purple he was indeed instrumental in contracting.

During these embassies, his character and bearing had drawn upon him the favourable notice of the emperor, who appointed him his secretary, and ultimately bestowed upon him the bishopric of Bamberg. In this position Otho soon became a man of mark. He was a zealous supporter of religion and of culture, an indefatigable redresser of grievances, and indeed an active labourer in every department of the Church's work. Nor did his personal standard fall below the mark at which he urged others to aim. His integrity, charity, and austerity were well and widely known. He had won very naturally the regard and gratitude of several popes.

Such a man was sure to be interested in the Pomeranian mission, and when Otho heard that Bernard was in Bamberg, he invited him to an interview, and listened carefully to the story of his defeated hopes.

Bernard pressed the bishop to address himself to the work in which he had failed, dwelling upon the effect likely to be produced on the Pomeranians by the splendid accessories which he had at his command. Boleslav, moreover, seconded these entreaties, pledging himself to provide whatever might be deemed necessary for the enterprise, and engaging to bear the expense it would entail.

Otho yielded at last to the solicitations of his

friends, being further encouraged by solemn bene-
dictions from Rome, besides the dignity of papal
legate, bestowed by Calixtus II.

His mind once made up, he lost no time in making
extensive preparations.

He took care to provide himself with costly presents,
such as the Pomeranian chiefs would be likely to
covet. He appointed seven ecclesiastics, besides
Ulric, his favourite chaplain, to the mission, and
secured the services of suitable attendants. Nor did
he omit to take with him abundant ecclesiastical
paraphernalia wherewith to furnish and embellish the
churches which he meant to build. In this provision
something of the man's characteristic determination
reveals itself.

On the 25th of April, A.D. 1124, the bishop and his
party started.

As long as they were in Bohemian territories they
trod on friendly ground. After a week's travelling
they reached Breslau, and thence passed on, by way
of Posen, to Gnesen, where they were received by
Boleslav himself. Many bystanders threw themselves
at the feet of the bishop, imploring his blessing.
The sovereign and the legate now conferred together
as to the course to be pursued, and a week was
spent by the outward-bound party in making final
arrangements. On the eighth day after reaching
Gnesen, all was ready. Waggons were laden with
the baggage and provisions, a store of Pomeranian
money was provided, interpreters, well acquainted
with the German and Slavonic languages, were in

attendance, and an armed escort was drawn up under
the command of an officer named Paulicius.

The cavalcade advanced into the dense forest which
lay on the border-land between Poland and Pomerania. Once before only, when some of Boleslav's
troops, bent on plunder, had braved its intricacies,
had this forest been penetrated from the Polish side.
The trees then cut down were the only guide to the
present travellers, for there was no track or pathway
of any kind; and so difficult was progress found,
that six days passed before the bishop and his people
reached the open country. They then found themselves on the banks of the river Netze, and in the
presence of the Pomeranian duke Ratislav, who was
attended by five hundred soldiers. The hearts of the
Polish ecclesiastics died within them at the aspect
of these warriors, who, flourishing their formidable
knives, hinted unmistakably at flaying suitable victims, or burying them in the ground up to their
necks. Night was rapidly advancing, and the whole
scene was calculated to intimidate the wayfarers, who
were however reassured after a time by the discovery
that no real harm was intended. After some discussion, the duke granted his sanction to Otho's proposed attempt at evangelizing the Pomeranians, and
without more ado, the party pressed forward again.

Pyritz was now their aim, to which town the road
lay across a district so devastated during the recent
struggles with Poland, that out of all its villages
only thirty inhabitants survived. These peasants
were interrogated on the subject of baptism, to which

I

they hastened to submit, being greatly alarmed at the soldiers who escorted the legate. Otho derived much satisfaction from the thought that though in this handful of peasants he contributed but a scanty first-fruits of his mission to the Church, yet their actual number, *thirty*, was a mystical one. For it was produced by multiplying the number of the Trinity by the number of the Decalogue.

On his arrival at Pyritz, one of the native religious festivals was in progress, and the town was thronged with visitors. The missionary party, therefore, decided on encamping for the night outside the walls. It was considered prudent to abstain from kindling a fire, or making any movement likely to attract attention, and the hours of darkness were most uneasily spent.

When daylight reappeared, the captain of the guard, accompanied by the ducal envoys, boldly entered Pyritz, and called a meeting of the leading inhabitants. He announced that a papal legate of rank and power, accompanied and escorted as became his position, awaited admission into the town. Persuasion and threats were adroitly mingled in his address, and the people, cowed by the show of authority, at length consented to receive the bishop. A procession, as imposing as Otho's resources permitted, was accordingly drawn up, and the Polish embassy marched into the town. The bishop no sooner reached a central position, where he could be heard with ease and to advantage, than he stepped forward, arrayed in his most splendid vestments, and disarmed all suspicion by an eloquent and affectionate address.

The people listened attentively, for this at least was a person widely different from Bernard the mendicant, of whose adventure at Julin they had heard. Yet, grand as he was, and stately as the retinue at his command, he seemed, by his own account, to have come a long and weary way for their sakes. It might be well to hear what he had to say.

For some little time the bishop and his clergy confined themselves to the work of teachers, but when the minds of the people were somewhat prepared for what was to follow, a fast of three days was proclaimed, and purification, by all available means, urged upon them. Baptism was then administered to more than seven thousand candidates,[1] to whom the nature of the vows which they were about to take upon them was clearly and impressively explained. Twenty days in all were devoted to Pyritz. The bishop then withdrew, leaving behind him some of his clergy.[2]

[1] For the details of this administration, and the decorum observed on the occasion, see Herbordi, *Vita*, ii. 15; cf. also ii. 19, 35.

[2] "All ye, my brethren," said this 'apostle of the Pomeranians,' in his farewell sermon, "who have believed in Christ, and have been baptized, have put on Christ. Ye are cleansed and pure, not through any deed of your own, but through the operation of Him into Whose Name ye have been baptized, for He has washed away the sins of the whole world in His Blood. Beware, then, of all contamination with idolatry; put your trust in God, Who is your Creator, and worship no created thing, but rather seek to advance in faith and love, that His blessing may come upon you and upon your children, and that, believing in Him, and adorning your faith by your works, ye may have true life through Him Who has called you out of darkness into His marvellous Light."

Cammin was the next halting-place. Here the efforts of the missionaries were much assisted by the wife of duke Ratislav, and forty days were spent in the work of evangelization. The duke himself renounced polygamy,—an example which produced a marked effect upon the people,—a church was built, and baptism administered as at Pyritz, only on a still larger scale. So far the earnestness of Otho had been his most effective weapon against paganism. It carried weight which equalled, if it did not exceed, the influence of the Polish soldiery behind him. But the way now grew rougher.

The baggage of the missionaries having been transferred from waggons to boats, they proceeded next to Julin, where Bernard had so injudiciously roused the fury of the inhabitants by assaulting one of their idols. The place was a very stronghold of pagan idolatry.

The boatmen respectfully advised Otho to anchor at some little distance from the town, and to avoid all possible stir, lest attention should be attracted, and entrance forbidden, before he had time to approach. They suggested that he should seek shelter for the night in a fort which had been built specially as a place of refuge or sanctuary for those hardly pressed by enemies. Creeping accordingly into this building in the dusk, Otho awaited the morning with no little anxiety. And indeed the day had scarcely broken before the fort was surrounded by an enraged mob, who threatened the whole party with death if they did not immediately depart. Argument was unavailing ; the people had lashed themselves into a fury which had no ear for reason, and it was only with much difficulty and peril that Otho and his suite contrived to escape. They were compelled, as it was, to break the bridge behind them, or they could not have regained their boats safely. Otho now withdrew to a prudent distance, and messages passed to and fro, in which the inhabitants learnt that the wrath of the duke might be expected on account of their behaviour, and after some consequent reconsideration they at last agreed that the bishop should be admitted within their walls, if Stettin first opened its gates to him. More than this promise to follow Stettin's lead was not to be extracted from the people of Julin, and the good legate accordingly resolved to try his fortunes at the place indicated.

At Stettin a landing was effected, but the inhabitants disdained both the missionaries and their errand. They did not scruple to hurl reproaches at Otho, declaring that they had seen many Christians who were both dishonest and untruthful, and that they preferred their own creed.

For two months the bishop vainly strove to remove the unfavourable impressions of Christianity entertained at this place. Gentle measures were of no avail. At last he resolved to report the conduct of the people to Boleslav, and a rumour of his intentions having spread through Stettin, they, like the townsfolk at Julin, began to reconsider their position. Finally they, as well as Otho, sent an ambassador to Poland, promising to accept Christianity if permanent peace might be granted to them and their tribute-money diminished.

Meanwhile the legate persevered. A cross was erected in the market-place, and he continued his exhortations in spite of discouragement and resistance. Now and then, but very rarely, he was cheered by a sign of success. Two young men of good position in Stettin, for instance, after listening with reverent attention to the bishop's teaching with reference to the " Resurrection of the body and the Life of the world to come," presented themselves voluntarily as candidates for baptism. After their admission to the Church, their mother encountered them in their white baptismal garments, seated at the feet of the bishop. To the intense surprise of all spectators, she fell at once on her knees, and thanked God that she had lived to see that blessed day. Otho himself, who was sitting at the time on a mossy bank outside the town, teaching, as was his wont, by the wayside, was profoundly impressed. And the conformity of this leading family to the new faith was instrumental in inducing others, of lower rank, to embrace it.

The messengers now returned from Gnesen, bringing help to Christianity in the shape of letters from Boleslav, which very soon wrought a change in the general attitude of the townspeople. His command was positive. They must accept Christianity and abjure paganism. When that was done, he, for his part, would grant them the petitions they had urged.

The next step was the destruction of the idols.

Otho and his clergy assailed them right and left, with axes and with clubs, and at first the natives of Stettin watched the audacious proceedings with awe and trepidation. But as temple after temple was demolished, and one image after another hewn in pieces, and still no harm befel the missionaries, their courage began to revive. It really seemed that these gods of theirs were incapable of striking a blow in their own behalf! how then, should they be expected to defend their worshippers? And so the people also fell to with a will, and soon four of the largest temples were destroyed, and their materials used for fuel. One of them, consecrated to Triglav the triple-headed, was rich in treasures. It contained bulls' horns tipped with gold, goblets of silver and gold, spoil of all kinds seized in battle. And all were tendered to the bishop by the people. But he, who, as they knew, was generous to prodigality, declined to receive, while he revelled in the pleasure of giving. He directed that all the valuables should be distributed among the inhabitants of the town, with the exception of Triglav's own triple head. This curiosity he sent to the pope.

Against every form of Slavonic superstition Otho waged war. The sacred horse, the holy oak, the spring of supernatural properties, all long revered by the people of Stettin, were stripped of their pretensions, and reduced to the level of ordinary animals, trees, and brooks. The only person of position who to the last remained obdurate, notwithstanding all that he heard and saw, was the heathen priest whose place it had been to attend to the sacred horse. He refused absolutely to change his creed.

A church crowned the market-place before Otho left Stettin, and when he again appeared before Julin, having paused on his way to preach and baptize at Garz and Lubzin, he found the people ready to meet him almost with open arms. They were quite aware of what had taken place at Stettin, and amply fulfilled their promise to be guided by it. Baptism was largely administered, and Julin was converted into a bishopric, to which Adalbert, one of the duke's chaplains, who had attended Otho on his expedition, was afterwards appointed. The chancels of two churches, moreover, were consecrated at Julin by the legate, who then repaired to Clotkowe, to Colberg, and to Belgrade, in succession. At all these places his efforts were blessed with considerable success. But winter was coming on, and after rapidly re-visiting the various scenes of his labours, and endeavouring to strengthen the newborn faith of the converts, whom he earnestly besought to aim at holiness of life, he turned his steps homewards, and arrived at Bamberg in February, A.D. 1125, after nearly ten months' absence.

The next two years found the good bishop absorbed in the manifold cares and labours of his own diocese. But he never ceased to be solicitous about the Pomeranians, and as soon as he could be spared from his post at home, he started again to visit them. This time, although his preparations were as elaborate and as costly as before, he bore their expense himself, instead of laying it to Boleslav's account. It is supposed

that reports had reached him of a pagan reaction in
Pomerania.[1]   But whether he was prepared for any
falling off, or not, he was soon confronted by a spectacle which could not fail to distress him.   His point
of entrance into Pomerania on this occasion was at
Demmin.   And here he met duke Ratislav returning
triumphantly from a war against the Leuticians, accompanied by a gang of prisoners, all destined to the
ignominy and suffering of slavery.   Otho however
expostulated earnestly with the duke, nor did he
plead in vain.

Still greater disappointments awaited him.   But
at present he concentrated his energies on one
important point.   A diet was held at Usedom on
Whitsunday, at which Ratislav—penitent, perhaps, for
his own backsliding in the matter of the slaves,—pre-
sided.   He argued at great length in favour of Christianity, and of the bishop as its representative, after
which Otho himself addressed the assembled chiefs,
expounding the doctrines associated with the day,
from the first Pentecostal outpouring of the Spirit, to
the indwelling of His blessed, secret influence, through
all time, in the hearts of men.   After this gathering,
where a great impression was produced, and a decree,
permitting the propagation of the true faith, was
passed, the clergy in attendance on the bishop were
sent forth, two and two, in different directions, as
heralds of the approaching episcopal visitation.

The public sanction accorded to Christianity at

[1] Hardwick, p. 225.

the diet of Usedom enraged the pagan priests even beyond anticipation.

Foreseeing that their present overweening influence with the people must inevitably wane, many of them determined at any rate to exert it to the utmost while it lasted, and they did not hesitate to threaten with death all those who should venture to receive the clerical representatives of the bishop.

Out of this resolutely hostile attitude of the priests grave difficulties soon arose, of which a single instance shall here be cited.

The districts to be traversed by Otho's messengers having been carefully distributed and assigned, the clergy started on their travels. Two of them, by name Ulric and Albin, arrived, in obedience to their instructions, at the town of Wolgast.

The hospitality of the Pomeranians was proverbial, and the arrangements of every house included, as a matter of course, a room kept in constant readiness for the accommodation of any guests who might present themselves without notice. As strangers, Ulric and Albin were accordingly welcomed with great cordiality by the wife of the burgomaster. But no sooner did the object of their visit transpire, than their hostess betrayed much agitation, and assured them that the present mood, not only of the priests, but of the people of Wolgast, was one with which it would be perilous to trifle. A special reason was found to exist for this unusual unanimity of adverse feeling.

One of the leading local priests had worked upon

the superstitious credulity of the inhabitants of the
town, for his own purposes, with a success altogether
disproportionate to the ingenuity of the artifice employed. Disguised, with the help of his white robes
of office, as a spectral figure, he hid himself in a
forest whose trees overhung and darkened the road
into Wolgast. A lonely peasant on his way home
was startled by the sudden appearance of a ghostly
figure just within the border of the wood, which
called to him in an unearthly voice, commanding
him to pause and listen. The soft gloom of a sum-
mer night favoured the design of the impostor. Far
from recognizing him, the terrified wayfarer firmly
believed that he beheld an apparition from another
world, and halted as he was desired, in a state of
abject alarm which effectually cancelled such reason-
ing powers as he possessed.

"Stand!" muttered the spectre, from the leafy
shadows, "stand! and hearken to what I say. I
am thy god! I am he that clothes the fields with
grass, and arrays the forests with leaves; without me
the fruit-tree cannot yield its fruit, nor the field its
corn, nor the cattle their increase. These blessings
I bestow on them that worship me, and from them
that despise me I take them away. Tell the people
of Wolgast, therefore, that they think not of serving
any other god but me, for no other can profit them,
and warn them that they suffer not these preachers
who are coming to their town to live."

The voice ceased, and to the relief of the unfortunate countryman the figure vanished into the

heart of the forest.   More than ever convinced that he had been harangued by one of the supernatural beings believed by the Slavonians to haunt the woods, the peasant made the best of his way into the town. Here his story soon attracted a crowd, and was unhesitatingly accepted as genuine by every hearer. The priest who had played the spectre so impressively presently himself slipped into the wondering throng, and—affecting intense curiosity—plied the man with question upon question, observing that every fresh detail thus extracted served to deepen the impression already produced.

Then, turning to the people, he exclaimed reproachfully, " Is not this what I have been telling you all the year long?   What have we to do with any other god ?   Is not our own god justly angry with us ?   How can we, after all his benefits, ungratefully desert him for another?   If we would not have him in righteous anger strike us dead, let us put to death these men who would seduce us from our faith ! "

Thus stimulated, the excitement of the population rose to fever-heat, and Ulric and Albin soon found that the burgomaster's wife had by no means exaggerated the danger of their position.   In spite of her fears, however, their kind hostess provided them with a safe hiding-place in her house for two days, after which Otho himself, numerously attended, and escorted by a detachment of troops large enough to intimidate the people, came to the rescue.   More than one chief who had assisted at the Usedom diet

accompanied him, and in the face of such a retinue
no enemy in Wolgast dared to lift a hand.

The customary mission-work accordingly began,
but proof was very soon furnished of the still dan-
gerously sensitive state of the popular temper. Some
of the clergy in the episcopal train thought fit to dis-
regard all warnings, and paid a visit of curiosity to
the pagan temples of the place. An angry crowd
followed them, threatening mischief if they persisted,
and the majority of the offenders at once retraced
their steps to the legate's quarters. One, however,
walked fearlessly into the temple of Gerovit, the god
of war, and before the mob had time to act he
reappeared, brandishing the sacred sword which no
mortal might touch and live. At this amazing
temerity the crowd fell back in horror, but a dis-
turbance followed, in which the pent-up enmity of
the pagans found vent.

But Otho, supported and assisted as he was,
proved too formidable a personage to defy. The
people receded by degrees from their hostile position, and their ignorant prejudices gave way, after a
while, to the new influence. Before the bishop took
leave of Wolgast, many came forward to receive
baptism, and the foundations of a church were actually laid.

Gützkow was the next scene of the episcopal visitation. Here Otho met messengers from Albert the
Bear, who offered his sword in support of the mission. But the bishop declined his services, being
accustomed steadily to avoid the employment of

force whenever it was possible. At Gützkow stood a pagan temple renowned for its size and its splendour, and the people pleaded long that this imposing building might be left standing, suggesting its conversion into a Christian church. Otho, however, feared the power of the law of association, especially in future and quieter times, when the excitement of novelty would have passed away. He therefore hardened his heart against the petitioners, and gave the word for the demolition of the temple, but he tempered his apparent severity by a promise to build in its place a church so beautiful as to supersede its attractions in every respect. This undertaking was duly carried out, and at the consecration of the new church the bishop preached an impressive sermon on the necessity of self-dedication to God, and the futility of all external offerings, however choice, unless the life brought forth fruit in the shape of such sacrifices as alone are well-pleasing to Him. Mercy, charity, forgiveness, truth,—these, he assured his hearers, must testify to the state of a man's heart before God, and every habit running counter to the free play of such virtues must be absolutely and finally abandoned. " Remember these words of the Lord's Prayer," said the earnest preacher, by way of illustration, " forgive us our debts *as we forgive our debtors.*"

The appeal wholly overpowered the governor of the district, Mizlav by name, who was present. He had been baptized at Usedom, and he now responded to the charge of the bishop by a practical proof of his own sincerity. He announced that he would at once release all his debtors then in confinement. " Here, then," said he, " in the Name of the Lord Jesus I give these men their liberty, that, according to thy words, my sins may be forgiven, and that dedication of the heart of which thou hast spoken may be fulfilled in me." One prisoner, however, probably detained under peculiar circumstances, was not set free with the rest. He was a Dane of noble birth, held by the governor as security for a personal debt of his father's, amounting to five hundred pounds. When the bishop heard that this single reservation marred the governor's noble act of emancipation, he became anxious for its removal, but he dreaded overtaxing the conscience of so fresh a convert, lest a reaction should set in. He contrived, nevertheless, that gentle and indirect recommendations should reach the ear of Mizlav, who, after no slight struggle, yielded. The captive was brought forth, and conducted to the altar of the newly-built church. Here Mizlav bestowed upon him his freedom, and uttered a devout hope that as he had remitted the debt of the Dane, his own sins might be forgiven him by his Father in heaven. This affecting scene was not without lasting effect on many among its spectators.

Space fails us to describe in detail all the adventures of the intrepid cross-bearers. But one of Otho's chief disappointments during his second visit to Pomerania, which must have gone far towards outweighing his many causes for encouragement, deserves a short notice. For it occurred at Stettin, where, in spite of the original obstinacy of the inhabitants, so much good work, as we saw, had been done. Paganism was found to have reasserted itself here with a virulence which not only grieved the bishop to the heart, but also so alarmed the clergy who attended him, that when, notwithstanding the discouraging reports which were afloat, he declared his intention of revisiting the place, not one volunteered to accompany him. The brave prelate thereupon resolved to go alone. Having committed himself to God in prayer, he accordingly started for Stettin. But he had no sooner actually moved in the perilous direction than some of his clergy, conscience-smitten for their cowardice, hastened after him, assuring him that, whatever might betide, they would indeed cast in their lots with his.

The town was found to be in commotion. A pestilence was raging, which the pagan party—who were doing their utmost to fan the heathen reaction into a still fiercer blaze—averred to be a sign of the wrath of their justly-incensed gods. The church built by Otho on his previous visit was attacked, and would have been remorselessly destroyed, but that one of the pagan ringleaders was suddenly disabled by a fit. This judgment was referred by the man himself, on his recovery, to the displeasure of the God of the Christians, and he prevailed upon his excited friends to leave the sacred building unmolested. In order, however, to be secure from all supernatural anger whatsoever, a pagan altar was reared within the church, and so the matter rested.

Bishop Otho appeared in the town during a lull in the general frenzy, which was due to the immediately previous arrival, from the island of Rügen, of a Pomeranian magistrate who had been baptized by him more than two years before, and had since been languishing in a Danish prison. This chief's return was singularly opportune. For the burden of the tale which he eagerly poured into the ears of the Stettin people was, that having fallen asleep in his dungeon one night, after a piteous prayer for deliverance, he dreamt with great vividness that Otho drew near to him, and signified that his petition was granted. Awaking, he found the door of his cell open, and immediately effected his escape as far as the sea-shore. Here he met with no hindrance. A boat lay on the beach, as if awaiting him, and in it he had safely accomplished his return to Stettin. Overwhelmed with thankfulness, he hung up the boat like a trophy at the entrance of the town, and so repeatedly and emphatically attributed his merciful liberation to the Christian's God, that his sentiments produced a marked effect upon the volatile and wavering townspeople.

The heathen faction, notwithstanding, made another desperate attempt. Through the agency of its leaders, the church, within which the bishop and his following had mustered, was suddenly surrounded, and instant death was threatened to those within. But Otho's self-possession did not for a moment forsake him. Placing himself at the head of his clergy, he ordered the church-door to be opened, and moved quietly out, bearing the uplifted cross, and chanting Psalms, into the midst of his assailants. His courageous demeanour no doubt preserved his life. Compelled to admire his manliness in spite of themselves, the pagans drew aside and let him pass, and danger was thus once more averted.

Witstack, the chief who had so lately eluded the Danish grasp, now urged Otho to make the most of the temporary advantage he had won, and to fix the following Sunday for a public address to the people. In the mean time he exerted himself, by every means in his power, to bespeak a large attendance and a general interest in the promised discourse.

Sunday came, and the bishop kept his word. Mounting the steps in the market-place whence magisterial proclamations were customarily issued, he delivered a powerful sermon to the assembled multitude, and was so far fortunate that a patient hearing was granted him. But he had barely ended his address, when a pagan priest, sounding an alarm upon a trumpet, loudly adjured the people at once to destroy this man who presumed to set their gods at defiance. The danger was urgent. Ready spears were instantly pointed, and the last moment of the bishop's life seemed indeed to have come. But again the would-be murderers were mysteriously impressed by the majestic and unbroken calmness of his demeanour. The spears were not launched. As Otho quietly confronted his foes without the shadow of a sign of fear, a spell fell over the assembly, and no man moved. The significant pause was only broken by the movement of the bishop himself; he went straight to the church, and there destroyed the heathen altar which defiled its precincts. It was a severe test of the power he wielded over the popular mind. But the issue was triumphant. A rapid revulsion of feeling took place in favour of so brave a man, and the tide of fanaticism turned in good earnest. After a long debate, it was finally agreed never again to hinder the advance of Christianity.

The Pomeranians were indebted to bishop Otho for temporal as well as spiritual benefits. Their audacity had sorely provoked duke Boleslav, of whose leniency in the matter of the reduced tribute-money they had taken unworthy advantage. Twice, since the yielding of that knotty point, had they conspired afresh against the Polish rule, and twice the duke collected an army, and prepared to take summary vengeance on his incorrigible subjects. But on both occasions Otho interposed, and succeeded in averting the impending punishment. Thus, persistently as the Pomeranians had clung to their idolatry, and weakly as they had returned to it, they could not withhold their admiration and their gratitude from their noble benefactor. They always felt —and at last were proud to feel—themselves the objects of his affectionate solicitude.

In the year A.D. 1128, Otho concluded a final round of ecclesiastical inspection in Pomerania, and after attending the imperial diet in Germany, he returned once more to his own diocese. With the exception of the island of Rügen, of whose stubborn devotion to paganism more will be said hereafter, no feature in the programme of evangelization which he had originally drawn up had been omitted. And even in the case of that obdurate island he would have risked any amount of personal danger, had a landing been found possible. He was only beaten back by the insurmountable barrier of absolute impracticability.[1]

Until his death, which occurred in the year A.D. 1139, the bishop's anxious care for his Pomeranian converts never flagged. Though unable to revisit the scenes so interesting to him, he continued at a distance to be the support and comfort, as he had been the originator, of the Pomeranian church. One of his last acts was a deed of kindness to some of its members. A band of Pomeranian Christians having been made prisoners during a sudden raid of foreign pagans, a quantity of valuable cloth was sent to their countrymen by the considerate bishop, with instructions that part of it should be applied to the purpose of securing the goodwill of the heathen chiefs—cloth being an article highly prized,—and the rest converted into money wherewith to ransom the unfortunate prisoners.

The figure of the zealous Otho stands out in strong and bright relief against the dark background of the times in which he lived. His character was one which would have been an ornament to an age of far riper civilization, and were he the type of the Slavonic missioners in general, instead of the remark-

[1] See page 145.

able exception to their rule, the conversion of the Slavs might truly have been sketched in fairer colours. For in him we find strength fused in gentleness, zeal tempered with discretion, courage illuminated by humility, and an earnestness of purpose by which all personal and worldly considerations were completely eclipsed.

CHAPTER VII.

CONVERSION OF THE WENDS AND LIEFLANDERS.

THE first attempts to illuminate the heathen darkness of Wendland date from the earlier half of the 10th century.

The tribes known as the *Wends* had found a home in the districts watered by the Elbe, the Oder, and the Saale, and were, even at this early period, tributary appendages to the German Empire.   But they cherished an undying hope of escaping from this dependent position.   Living constantly, as they did, on the watch for a chance of successful insurrection, they were not likely to regard a religion introduced and recommended by their conquerors, with a favourable eye.   From their hatred of their masters sprang a violent prejudice against their masters' creed, and the Christian missionary was an object of suspicion, because he was always associated with the political machinery behind him.   The clergy who visited Wendland, moreover, were, almost without exception, ignorant of the Slavonic language, so that a bridgeless gulf lay between them and the people with whom they attempted to deal.   Rightly or wrongly, they were also believed to be less anxious for the spiritual welfare of the Wends than for their own pecuniary interests.[1] Every now and then, the smouldering disaffection among the people broke into open flame, and while their brief triumph lasted they indulged themselves in slaughtering the clergy, and in demolishing all the churches within reach.

In the year A.D. 936, the death of the emperor Henry I., who had conquered the Wends, took place. With the accession of his successor, Otho I., the general aspect of affairs in Wendland brightened considerably. Bishoprics were created there, to which the emperor was careful to appoint zealous ecclesiastics, already experienced in missionary work elsewhere. These sees were gradually founded, at Havelburg, at Aldenburg, at Brandenburg, at Meissen, at Cisi, and at Merseburg, respectively. Agreeably to the decision of the Council of Ravenna, A.D. 967, they were all subjected to the archiepiscopal authority of Magdeburg, where one Adelbert, who had received his education in a monastery at Trèves, was installed as the first primate. The pall was bestowed upon him in A.D. 968. "One object of the emperor in urging the foundation of this new archbishopric appears to have been a wish to abridge the inordinate power of the see of Mayence." [2]

Boso, the bishop of Merseburg, who had been one of the emperor's chaplains, applied himself to the

[1] Robertson's 'History of the Christian Church,' iv. p. 90.
[2] Mansi. Quoted by Hardwick, 'Church History' [Middle Age], p. 128, note.

study of the Slavonic language, and mastered it sufficiently to be able to preach in it. His labours were
rewarded by the conformity of many hearers to
Christianity ; and, encouraged by his success, he proceeded to translate a few passages from the Liturgy
into Slavonic, but in this experiment he was somewhat disappointed, the people failing altogether to
apprehend its drift.

. The German clergy, who, as we have seen, were
men of a stamp vastly inferior to Adelbert and his
bishops, continued to tax and to irritate the Wends,
who were also becoming increasingly restive under
the political yoke of the Empire. At last, in the
year A.D. 983, long pent-up fury broke loose from all
restraints, and the people rose against their rulers
with terrible purposes of vengeance. So far was this
rising from a pagan demonstration, that it was headed
by Mistewoi, a chief who had fully embraced Christianity. Inflamed with anger on account of personal
grievances, he threw himself vehemently into the
insurrectionary movement. At Rethre, the centre of
a markedly heathen district, he rallied his ready
countrymen around him, and they fell savagely upon
Northern Germany, burning, slaughtering, and destroy-
ing, on the right hand and on the left. Wherever
Christianity had in any degree established itself, there
the rebels delighted to give freest play to their barbarity. It was long before the Church recovered
from the havoc wrought.

The time came when Mistewoi lamented with contrition the unworthy part he had played on this

occasion ; and although reparation was beyond his power, he was called upon to atone for his relapse by exile from his home. He died at Bardevik, while thus paying the penalty of his misdeeds.

The Christian principles of Gottschalk, the grandson of Mistewoi, were, in like manner, swept away for a time by a sudden flood-tide of passion. He had been educated, indeed, in a Christian school at Luneburg.[1] But the murder of his father, Udo, infuriated him. Forgetting everything except a wild craving for revenge, he called the Wends to arms, and ravaged Hamburg and Holstein. Having gratified his undisciplined passion, however, Gottschalk, like his grandfather, repented. He is said to have been struck and overwhelmed with remorse at the sight of one particular expanse of country which had been wasted by his own hand. Desolation brooded where once fair churches had graced the landscape, and suffering reigned in the stead of the industrious peace it had displaced.

Gottschalk solemnly vowed on the spot that he would thenceforward support and promulgate the religion against which he had sinned so grievously.

He is noted as the founder of the Wendish empire, which arose in the year A.D. 1047. Bent upon its enenlightment, he collected ecclesiastics from various parts, but chiefly from Bremen, which appears to have been a great clerical *rendezvous,* and "the point of departure for the northern missions."[2] The kindness

[1] Hardwick, ' Middle Age,' p. 128.
[2] Ibid., p. 129, note.

and hospitality of its archbishop, Albrecht, converted it into a real city of refuge, where ecclesiastics, whose lives in those wild times were always precarious, might confidently calculate on finding encouragement and welcome.

In inviting clergy to settle in his kingdom, Gottschalk by no means intended that their labours should supersede his own. He rather sought their co-operation and assistance. He himself, now an eager champion of Christianity, was instant in season and out of season, preaching, expounding, interpreting, and, in short, consecrating the intensity of his energetic character to the work of redeeming his subjects from their spiritual darkness. For nearly twenty years he toiled steadily on.

But it was in vain. The Wends loved their darkness better than their sovereign's light. They betrayed no inclination to espouse the religion for which he condescended to plead with them. To them it was offensive, if for no other reason, because it was ineffaceably tinged with the German element which they abhorred. So, with true Slavonic obstinacy, they clung to their idols. Against Gottschalk as a man, indeed, they could with difficulty find aught to allege; but as the contractor of an alliance with German princes, they hated him. The Wendish converts were too inconsiderable in number to resist the sullen wave of paganism which, seeming to gather strength every time it was forced to retreat, began at length to rise visibly higher and higher in opposition to the king.

It broke at last, and Gottschalk himself was one of the first victims swept away by its fury. He died under torture.[1] Ebbo, the priest at Lutzen, was murdered at the altar, and numbers of the clergy were stoned. These deeds of violence were the inauguration of a general rebellion. The wildest disorder soon prevailed, while the extirpation of Christianity was the aim, the hope, and the watchword of all malcontents, and perhaps the only object which they all with one accord agreed to pursue.

The life of John, bishop of Mecklenburg, was one of the many forfeited in this persecution. He was an Irish missionary who, after visiting Saxony, had been courteously received at Bremen by archbishop Albrecht, and by him introduced to king Gottschalk. This led to his nomination to the see of Mecklenburg. Bishop John had been one of the most successful toilers in the unfruitful vineyard of the Wends. But martyrdom crowned his labours. He was barbarously beaten with clubs, and derisively exhibited in town after town as a laughing-stock. At Rethre he was called upon to abjure Christianity. His refusal was absolute and unhesitating, upon which his tormentors cut off both his hands and his feet. Decapitation ended his sufferings, but his persecutors were not even yet satisfied. Casting his body ignominiously into the street, they mounted his head on a pole, and bearing it aloft to the temple of Radegast the god of war, they solemnly offered it to that deity.

[1] Hardwick, p. 129.

And now paganism reigned triumphant. Under Cruko, a chief whose detestation of Christianity was extravagantly bitter and relentless, almost every trace of missionary work vanished. Scarcely an echo was to be heard of the chorus of earnest voices which, despite discouragement and difficulty, had for so many years proclaimed glad tidings of great joy in Wendland. The anarchy was political as well as religious; the kingdom established by Gottschalk was a thing of the past. After some fifty years had elapsed, indeed, his son made an attempt to reinstate it on its former footing, as well as some efforts to revive downtrodden Christianity. But the Wendish Church owed its eventual re-settlement to the very influences which were fatal to the independence of the kingdom.

Albert the Bear and Henry the Lion—duke of Saxony—succeeded at last in subduing the country,[1] and under their auspices German colonists settled in the districts which had been exhausted and depopulated during the long years of tumult just past. Among these were many clergy, and most of the Wendish bishoprics were restored to existence.

But idolatry was still only very slowly displaced. The more northerly of the Wendish tribes adhered with more or less tenacity to their ancient creed, until the year A.D. 1162, when Henry the Lion utterly crushed the independence of the Obotrites,[2] whose resistance

---

[1] A.D. 1125—1162.

[2] "The former inhabitants of the present duchies of Mecklenburg, and the adjacent country, west, north, and south."—Talvi's 'Languages and Literature of the Slavic nations,' p. 300.

was the last among this division of the Slavonians, and
with other imperious conditions of peace dictated to
them the acceptance of Christianity.

Prior to this, however, these tribes were visited by
a missionary whose piety, courage, and nobility of
character endeared him, in spite of themselves, to
many who were far from friendly to his creed.

Vicelin—for such was his name—was born in a
village on the banks of the Weser, called Quernheim,
and educated at Paderborn. For three years he
"studied biblical and other literature at the university
of Paris."[1] Shortly after his ordination he heard of the
lack of zealous labourers in the Wendish mission-field,
and on applying in the year A.D. 1125 to the archbishop
of Bremen, he received a commission to preach the
gospel there. His first effort was at Lubeck, but the
political commotions there forbad either success or
perseverance. He then made the border-town of
Neumünster—formerly Faldera—his head-quarters,
and addressed himself to the work of enlightening
the districts north of the Elbe. The people with
whom he came in contact were demoralized by long-
endured misery. The country was wasted by con-
tinually-recurring war, and idolatry was the solitary
possession remaining to the inhabitants. Vicelin,
however, did not despair. Before long, he was the
head and centre of a religious fraternity, comprising
lay as well as clerical members, the avowed object of
whose lives was personal consecration to good works.
For nine years this devoted brotherhood strove with

---

[1] Hardwick, p. 226, note.

the surrounding heathenism. They prayed, they exhorted, they gave alms, they visited the sick, they whispered of the Power of the Cross in the ears of the dying. In evil report and good report Vicelin was constant to his post, and when the emperor Lothaire II. visited Holstein in the year A.D. 1134, he testified his appreciation of the work that had been accomplished by appointing the indefatigable pastor to the charge of the churches of Lubeck and Segeburg. This important commission was accompanied, moreover, by warm and gratifying words of encouragement.

But only three years afterwards, the Wends, recognizing in the death of the emperor a favourable opportunity for revolt, again took up arms. Churches and monasteries were attacked once more, and no Christian priest's life was safe. Vicelin was driven from his work, and was obliged to return to Neumünster, where he did his utmost to rally his distressed converts, whom he literally upheld by his cheerful hopefulness and faith. And, in fact, a break in the clouds did gladden his brave spirit after a few patient years. Adolph, count of Holstein, succeeded at last in bridling the irrepressible Wends, and Vicelin's church at Segeburg was once more his own. Fearing, however, that fresh commotions might at any moment arise, he removed his monastic community to Högelsdorf. Here he was helped by the cordial sympathy of Dittmar, a canon of Bremen, and found himself in a position to resume the many charitable works which had been so rudely suspended. The gates of his monastery stood open when a severe famine was at one time afflicting the people of the district. And as he dispensed the loaves and other kinds of charity for which the hunger-stricken sufferers clamoured, this servant of God took occasion to urge their acceptance of the Living Bread Who came down from heaven. Nor was he without hope that he had touched the hearts of some whose bodily wants he had relieved.

In the year A.D. 1148, Vicelin became bishop of Oldenburg, on the nomination of the archbishop of Bremen. A disagreement ensued between his patron and Henry the Lion, who would seem to have objected to the revival of this particular bishopric. Conceding that point, however, the duke insisted on his right to grant investiture to the freshly-appointed bishop. The archbishop demurred, considering that such a change in the position of the prerogative would involve a slight to the Church which he ought not to countenance. This dispute was very trying to Vicelin, who, as far as he was concerned, waived the matter in deference to the duke. But his chief attention was concentrated, as it had ever been, upon his work.

The pagan god Prone [1] was the special object of adoration among the unconverted in the neighbourhood of Oldenburg. Vicelin persevered in strenuous endeavours to wean its worshippers from their superstition, until he had the gratification of observing not only that their numbers were considerably diminished, but that their faith was fundamentally shaken. A church was built, and many new subscribers to Christianity flocked to it.

[1] Probably synonymous with *Perun*.

The pious bishop had at length the happiness of presiding over a steadily increasing community of the faithful, after his many toils, until his death, which took place in A.D. 1154.

And now the original Wends were by degrees displaced by German colonists, and the profession of Christianity became the rule rather than the exception, throughout the territories once known as Wendland.

The paganism of the Wends did not, as we have seen, gradually melt away in the genial warmth and light of Christianity. It was remarkable for its persistency, and when it finally did, after desperate struggles, succumb, it was to hard blows only. As the political power of the Wendish empire was broken up into fragments incapable of reunion, so the strength of its ancient faith was literally hacked and cut to pieces. And we cannot but notice that, when at last the remnants of its heathenism were too scattered and too insignificant ever to coalesce again, the people themselves were fast disappearing, and making room for races of a more pliable temperament.

We must now turn to another instance of determined hostility to innovation in matters of faith.

Otho of Bamberg, ultimately so successful in his Pomeranian crusades, had been completely baffled in one quarter, which from a distance had attracted his observation and kindled his enthusiastic desires to visit it. This as we have seen,[1] was the island of Rügen ; the Mona, as it has been called, of the Baltic Slavonians. Here, as in a fortress, Slavonic paganism

[1] Cf. pp. 131, 132.

seemed to have intrenched itself, with a dogged
resolution never to be dislodged.

So great was the dread inspired by the current reports of the ferocity of the Rügen heathen, that when
Otho with his usual intrepidity proposed and prepared to visit the island, only one among all his party
of attendants was to be found who was willing to
share the peril. Storm after storm prevented their
landing, and during the delay ominous rumours of
the pagan attitude in Rügen stole across the water.
The bishop's friends among the Pomeranian chiefs
then interfered. They assured the zealous missionary
that to land on the island would be to rush into the
arms of certain death.

Then Otho reluctantly gave way, and Rügen was
left to its paganism.

The towns of Stettin and Julin, scenes—as we saw
them to be—of some of the bishop's most effective
ministrations, were denounced as apostate by the
bigoted islanders, who never ceased to terrify their
inhabitants by threats of the severest vengeance.

The quarrel became permanent, and the Danes,
after a time, took part in it. In the year A.D. 1168,
Waldemar, king of Denmark, made common cause
with the Pomeranian chiefs, and the island was at last
subdued.

Thus, nearly forty years after the bishop of Bamberg had been obliged, in the interests of common
prudence, to abandon his hopes of converting its inhabitants, a path was cut by the Danish sword for the
tardy entrance of Christianity.

L

Rügen is at the present day one of the largest islands belonging to Germany. Its area comprises 440 square miles, and a strait, which at its narrowest point is a mile and a half wide, divides it from the mainland

Its greatest beauty consists in luxurious forests of beech-trees, which must have been celebrated in very early times for the richness of their verdure. Tacitus mentions the " sacred grove " in which the ancient inhabitants of the island worshipped Hertha, the goddess of the earth.[1] In the eastern part of Rügen various memorials of heathenism survive in the shape of granite slabs, generally supposed to have been altars. A " sacrificial stone" is also in existence there, in which a groove is bored for the purpose, it is conjectured, of carrying off the blood of the victims.

The time, then, had come for the admission of the light of truth to this fair island, nestling in its beech-woods, and shaded by the grave pine forests which darkly crowned its heights.

Bishop Absalom of Roeskilde, " a luminary of the Danish Church,"[2] took charge of the mission. He engaged to establish a Christian community in Rügen, and he kept his word. The island was in consequence eventually annexed to his diocese.

Arcona, the capital, only yielded after a long and stubborn siege. But the inhabitants, finding themselves

---

[1] It is however believed by many that Tacitus refers to Alsen, an island as large as Rügen, or larger, acquired by Germany in the Schleswig-Holstein war.

[2] Hardwick, p. 228.

overmatched by the Danish soldiery, made a virtue of necessity at last, and announced their readiness to adopt Christianity. They expressed at the same time a preference almost amounting to a stipulation, for the usages and forms of the Church of Denmark.

At Arcona stood the temple of Svantovit, already described.[1] It enshrined a colossal image of the deity, which was shrouded from the gaze of visitors by purple curtains, now worn with age. Bishop Absalom knew well that an exhibition of the impotence of Svantovit would speak more forcibly to the islanders than many sermons. He therefore lost no time, after entering Arcona, in bending his steps to the temple, accompanied by a picked band of axe-bearers, previously instructed in their duty.

An immense concourse of pagans attended the iconoclasts, expecting and hoping that their profane temerity would bring swift destruction upon their heads.

Absalom and his party, however, making very light of the majesty of Svantovit, hastily tore away the venerable curtains that screened him, and forthwith belaboured him about the feet with such vigour, that after a few strokes of their axes, a crash was heard, and the much-dreaded idol reeled, and fell heavily to the ground.

The spectators believed that they saw—their imaginations being prepared to see—the demon which had haunted the temple rush from the shrine at the moment of the idol's downfall, in the form of a

---

[1] See p. 23.

small black animal, which vanished as mysteriously as it had appeared.

Svantovit now indeed lay low. But even in the horizontal position he was appalling to the people of Rügen, among whom none could be found to give a helping hand in removing his prostrate figure.

They looked on in shivering fear, while ropes were attached to him, and he was dragged, amid derisive laughter, into the Danish camp. Here a speedy end was put to him, and the natives could not but draw their own conclusions, as they watched their vaunted god submitting unresistingly to be chopped in pieces for fuel.

And the last remnants of their awe died away when they beheld the Danish soldiers dining cheerfully on harmless food, which had nevertheless been cooked over fires kindled by the mutilated remains of Svantovit!

Bishop Absalom did not rest until all the other pagan temples in Rügen were destroyed, together with the images they inclosed. These idols were in some cases gigantic. One of them possessed seven heads, another five, and a third, four. And the height of one figure was so great, that when the energetic bishop took his stand upon its feet, his upstretched axe barely touched its chin.

The false gods being destroyed, root and branch, the foundations of Christian churches were next laid, and Danish clergy were summoned to Rügen, and posted in different parts of the island. No ecclesiastical levies were permitted to vex the people, and their hearty assent to the religion which they had so long resisted was finally secured.

The Lieflanders were a division of the Slavonic race which had freely intermingled with other branches of the Indo-European family, and with the Ugrian tribes of Fins.[1] They occupied the east coast of the Baltic as far as the gulf of Finland, and appear to have remained plunged in the darkness of ignorant superstition until late in the 12th century. They worshipped trees, they sacrificed human victims, they were spell-bound by the witcheries of sorcery, and altogether presented a most hopeless spectacle to the longing eyes of such missionaries as at last came in contact with them.

In the year A.D. 1186, a pious canon named Meinhard, who had been educated in Vicelin's monastery at Segeberg, sailed up the river Düna in a trading vessel from Bremen. At Yxkull the merchants had built a fortress to protect their commercial interests, and here Meinhard began his work. He earned the good graces of the people in the first instance, by assisting them in temporal matters.

---

[1] "Of the Fins on the Baltic, the most western locality is Courland, for thus far do Fins or Ugrians extend in the direction of Prussia. In Courland, however, the undoubted natives are Letts of the Lithuanian family, and the name that these Lithuanian Letts give to the Fins under notice is *Lief*. No definite account can be given of their origin; for, though *Lief* is a name which we may reasonably expect to find in *Livonia* (or *Lieflana*), it is not the one we look for in Courland." The *Liefs* gave the name *Livonia* to that country.—Dr. Latham's 'Russian and Turk,' p. 244.

Helped by his advice when suddenly attacked by
some crafty foe, and taught by him how to build a
stronger and better fort to defend their trade, they
conceived a respect for the venerable ecclesiastic's
talents, and listened so tractably to the spiritual
injunctions with which he ventured to accompany his
worldly wisdom, that Meinhard was overjoyed. He
administered baptism to several of his new friends,
and founded at Yxkull the first Livonian church.

On announcing his success to Hartwig, the archbishop of Bremen, he was rewarded by appoint-
ment to the see of Yxkull, which "was secured
to the province of Hamburg by the grant of Pope
Clement III., in the year A.D. 1188."[1]

But the joy of the sanguine Meinhard was short-
lived. During his visit to Bremen, which was undertaken expressly to report the satisfactory condition of
his converts, the people of Yxkull lightly forsook the
vows which they had lightly taken, and on the return
of the newly-created bishop, he found, to his chagrin,
that paganism had recovered its full force, and that
scarcely a vestige of his work had stood its ground.
Nor did the charm of his personal presence reclaim the
backsliders. They were now as devoted to their ancient
deities as if they had never heard of a purer faith.

The efforts of Meinhard were presently seconded
by Theodoric, a Cistercian monk, but he was unfortunate enough to excite the ill-feeling of the Lieflanders by most unexpected and innocent means.

---

[1] Hardwick, p. 229, note.

He cultivated some land near Yxkull so successfully
that the inhabitants were childishly indignant at the
superiority of his crops to their own. In a fit of
jealousy they vowed to sacrifice him to their gods.
But when they sought oracular sanction, the omens
were unfavourable, and on that account Theodoric's life
was spared. The superstitious fancies of the people,
however, were soon set in motion again. They next
suspected him to be mysteriously connected with
powers beyond their ken, and he was declared to be
responsible for an eclipse of the sun which disturbed
their equanimity. Finally, he left the country, de-
spairing of success, at any rate, by gentle means.
Meinhard, also deeply dejected, died at his trying post
in the year A.D. 1196.

Berthold, an abbot from Lower Saxony, was the
next volunteer. He began by a prodigal distribution
of presents, hoping so to ingratiate himself with the
flippant Lieflanders. But their toleration of him
lasted only while his gifts lasted, and he was insulted
as menacingly as Bernard had been at Julin. He
withdrew in resentment, but only to return at the
head of an army which Innocent III. had placed
at his disposal, wherewith to quell the insolence of
these remote heathen. An engagement took place, in
which Berthold fell, but the Lieflanders were compelled
to submit to a military force against which they felt
they had no power. Again they promised to be
Christians, and many received baptism in apparent
sincerity. But no sooner had the crisis passed, and
the soldiery departed, than the mantle of dissimula-

tion was again flung aside. The clergy who had been left in charge of the mission fell victims to the vengeance of the fickle populace, and not a few of the freshly baptized Lieflanders threw themselves frantically into the Düna, in the wild hope that its waters might obliterate the effects of their baptism.

But these obdurate tribes were not long left to their headstrong heathenism.

The next Livonian crusader was a priest from Bremen, Albert von Apeldern by name. He came with a considerable army at his back, and attended by a fleet of twenty-three ships. Deeming Yxkull too insecure a spot to be the seat of a bishopric, he made preparations for building the city of Riga, to which place the see was transferred in the first year of the 13th century.

The success of Albert among the Lieflanders was so indifferent and so fluctuating, that he came before long to a conclusion of some importance, which he forthwith dutifully communicated both to the emperor and to the pope. This opinion was, that no permanent effect would ever be produced in the country until the people were overawed by resident military. Desultory armed descents upon them, however authoritative, produced no lasting results, for as soon as the armies were withdrawn they abandoned themselves to their habitual reckless persecution of all that was good. But if the force they feared dwelt continually among them, their periodical excesses would be impossible. Moreover, if well-conducted soldiers could be introduced into the country and incorporated with the inhabitants, some benefit might be gleaned from a moral example combined with physical power. The soundness of this advice was proved in the sequel. It took practical shape in the establishment of a knightly order, whose chivalry, purity, and courage did, to a great extent, accomplish what Albert desired. This brotherhood was known as *The Order of the Sword*. Its members, who recognized the Virgin as their special protectress, were bound to celibacy, chastity, and sobriety, as well as to regularity in attendance at mass, and they swore to resist and break down heathenism with swords for ever drawn in defence of the Cross.

Such lands as they conquered in fair fight with the pagans they were entitled to keep. And to the crusade against heathendom they were committed so long as a single heathen remained unsubdued.

For more than twenty years the struggle went on. But the pagan resistance grew gradually fainter. German settlers and German influence worked here, though so tardily, as they had worked elsewhere.

The exertions of " The Order of the Sword " extended into Esthonia,[1] Semgallen, and Courland. How far the " conversions " proudly recounted by these valiant defenders of the faith were more than superficial cannot indeed be said. But, at all events, nominal Christianity was widely planted by their swords. And they were able to point to the bishop-

---

[1] "*Estonia* being but a Latin form of *Estland*, i.e. 'the Eastern Land.' Like Courland and Liefland, it was conquered by the Knights of the Sword. The serfs—in Estonia—were almost wholly Fin."—Dr. Latham's 'Russian and Turk,' pp. 245, 246.

rics of Revel, of Dorpat, and of Pernau, as strong-
holds of truth, whose creation, support, and defence
were entirely due to the wholesome and respectful
awe inspired by their name.

Four years after the removal of the original Livonian
see to Riga, an effort was made to awaken the interest
of the ignorant people in Scriptural history by means
of a Miracle Play. The Lieflanders, however, though
much impressed by the adventures of such heroes as
David and Gideon on the stage, were not without a
suspicion that mischief to spectators might lurk behind
the fascinations of the drama. When on one occasion, the army of Gideon was represented in the act of
assailing the Midianites, the performers found themselves suddenly deserted by the public. Believing
that the assault on Midian was but a prelude to an
attack on themselves, the assembled beholders fled
in a body, nor was it found practicable to reassure
them.

The following winter, archbishop Andreas of Lund
occupied himself in expounding to the people, in their
own language, the book of Psalms. He was encouraged by various signs of interest among his audience,
and a hope sprang up, which proved to be well founded,
that the worst was over, and that the scenes of the
past would never repeat, though they might for some
little time reflect, themselves.

Every inch of the way which the Cross had made
had been disputed, lost, recovered, and forfeited again,
times without number. So anxious had Innocent III.
been as to the result of the Livonian mission, that

when Berthold was collecting an army for his second
expedition, the pope recommended the volunteers
for a pilgrimage to Rome to change their course,
and turn their steps to these northern wilds. Great,
therefore, were the general gratitude and relief when
the long-hardened Lieflanders could at last be
reckoned among the inhabitants of Christendom.

CHAPTER VIII.

CONVERSION OF PRUSSIA AND LITHUANIA.

"It was the area between the rivers Vistula and Niemen," writes Dr. Latham, "that constituted the old Prussian domain." The language spoken there in the 13th century "was a form of the Lithuanic. We know this, because it survived the independence of the nation; and a kind of catechism in it, of the date of the Reformation, has come down to us. Moreover, there is the account of, at least, one traveller who visited the country, and came in contact with the native old Prussians. What proportion it bore to the rest he does not say. But he tells us that he heard them converse in their own mother tongue, and that he was present at a ceremony, which he describes, of a purely pagan character, a statement which we may readily believe; for *the obstinacy with which the Lithuanians in general held to their original creed was a notable characteristic of the race.*" [1]

The italics are not Dr. Latham's, but some emphasis seems appropriate on an observation which, though it bears particularly on a division of the Slavonic race not yet noticed in this treatise, yet tallies so completely with our experience, so far as we have examined them, of the national characteristics.

[1] 'Russian and Turk,' p. 321.

From the same writer we learn that the two traditionary
founders of the Prussian nation were *Wundewut* and
Brut, or *Bruten*.   In alluding to the eleven or twelve
subdivisions of the Prussia of the 13th century, he
remarks that " nearly all these had their eponymus in
the twelve sons of Wundewut," their primeval priest-
king.   The ancient Prussians were devout worshippers
of the powers of nature, and besides a variety of
minor deities, they held three gods in profound and
especial veneration.   These were *Perkunos*,[1] the lord
of the thunder, *Potrimpus*, the god of corn and fruit,
and *Pikullos*, the president of the infernal regions.
The name of Perkunos " may be found in the Lithuanic songs of the present time ; while, even in West
Prussia, '*Pakul*' is the name for the devil."[2]   In all
representations of Perkunos, the head was wreathed
in flame, while the expression of the face was fierce
and stern.   Potrimpus, on the other hand, was pic-
tured as a smooth-faced youth, crowned with wheat-
ears and green leaves.   Pikullos was of solemn aspect.
His beard was snow-white, his countenance was pale,
and his eyes downcast.[3]

[1] *Perun*, again, under another name.

'Russian and Turk,' p. 321.

[3] Prof. Max Müller observes, with regard to the plurality of
pagan divinities [in his ' Lecture on the Vedas '], that one god
was not considered to be limited in power by the pretensions of
another, and that the idea of superiority or inferiority in rank
was in total abeyance.   "Each god is felt " to be "a real
divinity, supreme and absolute, without a suspicion of those
limitations which, to our mind, a plurality of gods must entail
on every single god."—'Chips from a German Workshop,'
vol. i. pp. 27, 28.

No town or village was unprovided with a temple of greater or less pretension. But the national centre of the faith was at Romove, where the sacred oaks grew, and veiled statues of the several deities were placed. Romove was also the dwelling-place of the chief pontiff, a personage held in such extraordinary reverence, that for his sake, not only all his relations and connections, but even his officials, were accounted sacred. The subordinate members of the priesthood also ruled the minds of the people with an absolute and unquestioned sway. They were all celibates, and they had both the power and the will to require periodical human sacrifices, usually in the service of the gods Potrimpus and Pikullos.

Three wives were allowed to each native Prussian, but they were regarded purely in the light of slaves, and self-immolation was expected of them in the case of their husband's death. Human life, indeed, was but lightly esteemed. All the daughters in a family except one, were destroyed in infancy, or sold; and the aged and infirm, the sick and the deformed, both young and old, were unhesitatingly put to death. Not only were the wives of a man required to die because he was dead, but his slaves, his horses, hounds, hawks, and armour, were burnt in the flames which consumed his corpse.

Thus the paganism of the Prussians was regularly systematized, and planted so firmly among them that its roots were intertwined with their deepest affections, and they did not scruple to display the most rancorous hatred to the new faith, of which, from time to time, rumours floated to their ears.

One of the first missionaries who had ventured to land in this hostile country was Adelbert of Prague, of whom we have already spoken.[1]

He arrived at Dantzic in the year A.D. 997, escorted by a detachment of Polish soldiers furnished by Boleslav I. Presuming on the passive attitude of the Prussians, who did not prevent his landing, he dispensed—prematurely, as the event proved—with the protection of the ship in which he had arrived. Accompanied by a priest called Benedict and a pupil of his own, he started in a small boat, at the mouth of the river Pregel, to make the most of the footing he had gained in the country.

But while he was preparing to land, after a while, on the river-banks, a sudden attack was made by the natives, and Adelbert was struck so violently with an oar, while in the act of chanting the Psalms, that he fell, completely stunned, to the bottom of the boat. Escaping across the river, the missionaries eventually succeeded in effecting a landing on the opposite shore. But it was in vain that they appealed to the inhabitants of this district to grant them at least a hearing. Though one of the native chiefs himself called upon Adelbert for an explanation of his appearance and his errand, the bishop's address was speedily cut short by derisive shouts of defiance. "These are the fellows," cried one man, speaking for the rest, "who cause our crops to fail, our trees to decay, our herds to sicken. Depart! or expect instant death!"

---

[1] See pp. 69, 73, 74, 75.

Much discouraged, the missionary party withdrew, and turned their steps reluctantly towards the coast. Adelbert, however, indulged a hope that the prejudices of the people might in time be overcome, particularly if the clerical dress, which seemed to give great offence, were abandoned, and the direct work of evangelization postponed awhile. After living among the people as industrious laymen long enough to disarm their suspicions, he thought that a way might gradually be opened for the Gospel by indirect means. But these fond schemes were never realized. The bishop and his friends were surprised in a dark wood, where they had paused for refreshment and sleep, by a band of angry Prussians, and before Adelbert had time to defend himself, he died, pierced by seven lances, but endeavouring to the last to rally the fortitude of his companions.

Eleven years after this tragic conclusion of the first attempt to carry the Word of Life into Prussia, a second was made by Bruno, a chaplain of the emperor Otho III. A picture of St. Boniface, the apostle of Germany, which he saw at Rome, was said to have inspired him with a longing to preach the Gospel to the Prussians.

Pope Silvester II. having duly commissioned him accordingly, and sanctioned his consecration as regionary bishop of Magdeburg, Bruno set out for Prussia. But before a single year had passed, he and his whole party, which consisted of eighteen persons, fell a prey, like the zealous bishop of Prague, to the vindictive hatred of the people.

Nearly 200 years now passed away, during which the struggles with Poland deepened and strengthened the Prussian antipathy to Christianity. Identifying the sacred cause with the pressure of a yoke which they resisted desperately and loathed intensely, the people could not be induced even to tolerate a rehearsal of its pleadings. In the year A.D. 1207, indeed, a Polish abbot named Gottfried, seconded by a monk who sympathized in his anxiety for the salvation of all men, did succeed in catching the attention of a few Prussians. But he was of the hated race of Poles, and his voice was soon silenced. Convinced by the revengeful murder of his friend the monk, that the passion of the people was only thinly veiled, and ready at any moment to break upon his own head, he sadly concluded that the work of winning them was hopeless, and ceased to expostulate with them.

Three years afterwards, however, in A.D. 1210, a zealous monk called Christian arrived in Prussia from a Pomeranian monastery not far beyond Dantzic.

Pope Innocent III. authorized his mission, which for four years was conducted, if not successfully, at all events in comparative freedom from molestation. At the end of that time Christian presented himself in Rome with two converted Prussian chiefs, to whom he pointed as the firstfruits of a stubbornly unproductive field, garnered only after much toil and almost incredible difficulty.

Much gratified, the pope raised Christian to the episcopacy, and assigned to him a diocese in the arena of his late labours.

M

Papal admonitions were at the same time delivered
to the dukes of Poland and Pomerania, in whose
oppressive administration Innocent III. did not fail
to discern a grave hindrance to the spread of Christianity in Prussia.[1]

The new bishop now returned eagerly to his
work. But before long his hopes were heavily over-
clouded.

The pagan faction of the opponents to Polish influence in Prussia, roused by some fresh provocation,
burst once more into overt fury, all the more deadly
for its recent suppression. The courage of the very
converts failed them under the burden of taxation
which, in spite of the pope's injunctions, grew heavier
and more irritating every day. A general rising took
place. The pagans, unable to distinguish between
Christianity itself and the political system which un-
worthily degraded it into a mere tool for the com-
passing of ambitious ends, rushed upon all outward
and visible signs of the alien creed. Converts were
put to death, the seats of missionary effort were
ravaged, and nearly 300 churches and other sacred
buildings were destroyed.

The territories of Conrad, duke of Massovia, having
been wasted by the infuriated Prussians, he exerted
himself, with the important support of the pope, to
bring crusaders upon the scene. The "Order of
Knights Brethren of Dobrin" first strove to reduce
the rebels to order. But this body was found unequal

---

[1] Hardwick, 'Middle Age,' p. 231, note 13.

to the task. The "Order of Teutonic Knights," allied or amalgamated with the "Order of the Sword," whose work we watched in Liefland, then addressed themselves to the arduous undertaking. This fraternity had been originally organized for the purpose of defending German pilgrims on their way to the Holy Land. But now that the general enthusiasm for the old crusades had considerably abated, a new channel for the energies of brave adventurers was found in the Prussian intrenchments of heathenism.[1] For fifty years the sword was scarcely sheathed. Though violently opposed by the people, and detested by those who had hitherto enjoyed a monopoly of authority over them, the military Orders proved ultimately irresistible. Slowly and steadily · they cut their way into the very heart of Prussia, marking and guarding their onward road by strongly-built castles, round which clustered communities of German settlers. Such were the towns of Culm, Thorn, Marienwerder, and Elbing.

[1] "In the midst of this misery—the pestilence which raged during the siege of Acre—a few German merchants, from the coasts of the Baltic, sought to mitigate suffering by running up the sails of their ships as tents for the sick and dying. The happy results which followed their work led to an organization similar to that of the Orders of the Temple and the Hospital. Like those Orders, the Teutonic Knights rose to power and distinction. With the failure of the Crusades in the East, the Order was transferred to the more forbidding regions which had sent forth its founders, and their crusade was turned against the heathen of the Lithuanian, Prussian, Esthonian, and other tribes. They preached the Gospel with the sword."—Cox's 'Crusades,' p. 122.

The authority of the Teutonic Knights was practically unlimited. They deemed themselves the representatives of the pope, and for the compliance of Germans and Prussians alike they laid down rules, from which the slightest deviation was absolutely forbidden.

Within the territories which they commanded, baptism was literally the solitary passport to freedom. The convert might indeed call himself a freeman as soon as the baptismal waters had bedewed him, without further impediment. But the pagan who, fondly clasping his ancient idols to his heart, refused to be baptized, was a mere item among his master's goods and chattels. Some of the obdurate fled into Lithuania,[1] but the majority remained, to be crushed and coerced by slow degrees. In the year A.D. 1243, the pope partitioned the heathen countries thus laboriously acquired, into the bishoprics of Culm, Pomerania, and Ermeland. Each of these was again distributed into three parts, one of which was under the control of the bishop as its feudal lord, while the other two acknowledged the authority of the knights of the Order.[2]

Churches and religious houses now rapidly multiplied, and before the general diffusion of light the dark customs of paganism began to retire, to all appearance, finally discomfited.

Polish laws were put into force in Prussia, and the popes were urgent in their recommendation of

Hardwick, p. 232, note 4.   [2] Ibid., p. 232.

gentler measures than those hitherto employed. The country was divided into parishes. A careful provision was made for the education of Prussian children, and pious Dominican monks devoted themselves to the consolidation of the work of conversion, which in a large majority of instances had been equally superficial and arbitrary.

But even yet, though hunted and tortured, disabled and subdued, the spirit of paganism lived. Eight or nine years passed by, and then its crippled existence was suddenly announced to those who had believed it to be extinct. In a struggle with the Lithuanians in the year A.D. 1260, the Teutonic Knights were beaten ignominiously back, and eight brethren of the Order were captured. These prisoners were burned alive, as an act of homage to the heathen divinities.

The encouragement was enough. Prussian paganism instantly revealed itself again. With such strength as it possessed it fell once more upon the clergy, murdering and plundering them, and upon all the churches and monasteries within reach. These buildings were remorselessly destroyed.

But the knights took terrible vengeance. All the favours which had been extended to the Prussians on their submission to Christianity were revoked. The offending chiefs were degraded to the position of serfs; hosts of crusaders poured into Prussia to the assistance of the knights, and for twenty-two years no quarter was shown to any remnant of heathenism. At last, bathed in blood, the country surrendered an undivided allegiance to Christianity, as personified by the Teutonic Knights.

The Order now reigned supreme. Its members took precedence of the bishops in all matters of authority. The episcopal sees, indeed, were usually filled from its ranks, which embodied a threefold power,—military, political, and ecclesiastical.

A passing reference has just been made to the wild rebellion in Lithuania against the encroachment of the Teutonic Knights. That the inhabitants of this country were formidable warriors we may infer from the remark of Henry, the early historian of Liefland, "that his countrymen were as lambs to wolves in respect to the Lithuanians."[1]

We find, as has been anticipated on an earlier page,[2] that they offered a more solid, if not a more dogged, resistance to Teutonic influences, than any of their neighbours. "Lithuania and Samogitia are, as they were always, Russian or Polish, rather than Teutonic."[3] Longer even than the other branches of the Slavonic family, they gloried in the gloom of paganism. It was also, perhaps, in their case, of a deeper and more baleful shade than elsewhere. In Lithuania the idolatrous instinct did not content itself with revering the heavenly bodies, or the deities in which here, as among the Prussians, the forces of nature were believed to enshrine themselves. A much less restricted form of worship was prevalent.

[1] 'Russian and Turk,' p. 326.
[2] See page 156.
[3] 'Russian and Turk,' p. 327.

Lizards and serpents were not only venerated, but actually propitiated by human sacrifices. Thus a mission among the Lithuanians was likely to be baffled by a grosser idolatry, and by a bolder defence of it, than had been found in other countries.

About the time when schools were beginning to be established in Prussia, and during the delusive lull in the heathen activity of that land already noticed, a son of a Lithuanic chieftain seems to have come in contact with Christianity, and to have embraced it heartily. His name was Mindove, and a Dominican monk, called Vitus—perhaps one of the many labourers in Prussia—repaired to Lithuania, by the desire of Pope Innocent IV., in the hope of doing something towards dispelling the dense spiritual darkness of its people. The undertaking failed, however, and for nearly one hundred and thirty years there is no record of any missionary work in this benighted region.

But in the year A.D. 1386, the Lithuanian chief Jagal, who had inspired the Poles with a dread of his very name, agreed to become their ally instead of their enemy. He attached a single condition to each side of the contract; the young queen of Poland, Hedwige, should be espoused to him; and he, on his part, would bring Lithuania within the fold of the Church.

To this proposal the Poles made no objection, and Jagal was accordingly baptized at Cracow, and received the name of Vladislav. He then proceeded to Wilna with his queen, attended by a band of

Polish missionaries under the direction of Vasillo, a Franciscan monk.

Christianity having been solemnly accepted as the national creed, these ecclesiastics, in conjunction with the archbishop of Gnesen and the bishop appointed to the newly created see of Wilna, exerted themselves to extinguish the grossest and most repulsive of the pagan practices.

Images were broken to pieces, sacred groves cut down, holy fires quenched, and the serpents and lizards hitherto held divine publicly destroyed. The Lithuanians looked on, awestruck at first, and acquiescing only by compulsion in the high-handed proceedings of Vladislav. He personally took the lead in all missionary work, for which his acquaintance with the native dialects qualified him to a degree unattainable by the Polish clergy. He translated the Creed, the Lord's Prayer, and other instructive elementary formulas into the language of the people, and, in many cases, beguiled his subjects to baptism by the present of a white woollen garment, which appears to have been highly valued.[1]

As at Kief, the candidates were assembled on the banks of rivers, and there immersed or sprinkled in large companies, a single name, such as Peter or Paul, being often assigned to an entire division of converts.

The Christianity thus administered by prescription was not more deeply implanted in the hearts of the

---

[1] Döllinger, iii. 286.

Lithuanians than it had been among other quondam pagans, by a similar method.

In spite of the orders of the grand duke, they remained in many quarters secretly addicted to the superstitious habits which they had formally renounced. As late as "the middle of the 15th century serpent-worship was still dominant in many districts. And traces of heathenism are recorded even in the 16th century."[1]

In the year A.D. 1413, a Lithuanian ecclesiastic named Withold, though but slenderly informed himself, endeavoured to carry such light as he possessed into the darkness enveloping the Samaites.[2] These tribes had already been the object of missionary solicitude, during the ascendency of the Teutonic Knights. But the efforts then made to reach them had languished and expired without visible fruit.

Withold, however, backed by the approval and assistance of the grand duke, succeeded in winning at least a foothold for Christianity.

The town of Wornie, or Miedniki, which had been recently built, became the seat of a bishopric, to which the energetic priest was elevated. He was sorely tried by the tendency to total relapse which prevailed among his people. Much obscurity clouds the actual results of his labours, nor can the date of the real and final conversion of these tribes be accurately fixed.

[1] Hardwick, p. 337, note 11. See his references therein.
[2] Perhaps identical with the wild Samoeids, "a section of the Ugrian race."—Hardwick, p. 338, and note 2.

It remains to glance at the Laps, in whose dwelling-place on the confines of the Arctic circle Christianity was very tardily welcomed.

So far from comparing unfavourably, in point of natural characteristics, with less remote and more civilized nations, the inhabitants of Lapland have been found, by those who cared to interest themselves in them, to possess not a few sterling qualities, and in consequence have earned a fair reputation among the travellers whose curiosity has led them to brave the rigours of so unkind a climate.

Theirs, for example, is the conspicuous honesty which we have seen also characterizing the early Pomeranians. Even at the present day, scarcely any precautions are taken for the protection of their houses or property, and a general spirit of trust appears to prevail among themselves. This is the more noteworthy, because the Laplanders are naturally by no means either incautious, or disposed to confide in strangers. The reverse, rather, is the fact. For so few visitors find any inducement to land on their shores, that the normal attitude of the natives towards foreigners is one of somewhat marked distrust, based, to all appearance, on wonder and doubt as to the possible object of their visit. It has even been observed, with reference to the noticeable absence of crimes of violence among these people, that fear, begotten by suspicion of a stranger, is almost the only operating motive to which any exceptional deed of bloodshed has ever been traced. It is probably also to this distrustful feeling that the

neglect of the virtue of hospitality, of which Laplanders are often accused, may be referred.

Rarely carried to excess either in sentiment or in
practice, we find the Lap free alike from what my be
called the graces and the failings of enthusiasm.
This negative peculiarity may doubtless be safely
ascribed, in some degree, to the ungenial atmosphere
and the monotonous conditions in which his life is led.
But it is impossible to overlook the thread of connection between the natural traits of the Laplander,
even of modern times, and the features of the general
Slavonic character, as roughly sketched in the preliminary pages of this volume. It was there stated,
that although under pressure the early Slav showed
himself capable of considerable bravery, yet his
courage was more passive than active, requiring to be
roused into movement rather than kindling spontaneously from instinctive warmth of temperament.
And attention was drawn in the same place to the
great powers of endurance with which the Slavic races
were justly entitled to be accredited.

Side by side with these remarks it will be interesting to place the following reflections of a traveller in
Lapland, bearing date about fifty years ago.

" The Laplanders are, without doubt, of a very
peaceable and inoffensive disposition, rarely engaging
in quarrels, or hurried to any extremes by excess of
passion. A proof that their general tempers are not
violent or sanguinary, may be adduced from the circumstance that they never make use of their knives
for revengeful purposes, and that, though constantly

provided with these formidable weapons, which are worn round their waist, no instance occurs of their drawing them when they happen to fight.

" The Laplander of the present age is no soldier; but it ought not to be asserted, though he may be deficient in the qualities requisite to constitute one, that he is utterly destitute of courage. Courage comes and goes; shows itself in one thing and not in another; owes its birth in very many instances to custom and habits of life; and is frequently mistaken for insensibility. If passive courage consists in the patient endurance of hardships, the Laplander has a just claim to it; and if undaunted exposure to danger constitutes active courage, he is not the less entitled to the possession of this also." [1]

Missions to Lapland were organized in the first half of the 14th century, nor were they by any means unproductive of effect.[2] But Christianity was not generally received until two hundred years later.

Among these simple people, engrossed in their fishing expeditions and their breeding and hunting of reindeer, legend in some of its quaintest forms was early rife. Here and there it presents a groundwork

---

[1] 'A Winter in Lapland and Sweden.' A. De Capell Brooke, pp. 163, 164, 165.

[2] The paganism of ancient Lapland was of a complexion too similar to the superstitions already noticed in other Slavonic countries, to need any separate description. Witchcraft enslaved the population here, as elsewhere; and numerous deities were propitiated by periodical sacrifices. Mountains were always chosen as the sites for altars, and were consequently held in great veneration.

into which we fancy, as we read, that not a few of the aspirations of Christianity would readily weave themselves.

One of these fables may here with some advantage be inserted, for in it we catch a distant and feeble echo of more than one truth most familiar to our own ears from childhood onwards.

"A long time ago there lived a Tadibi, whose name was Urier. He was a Tadibi of the Tadibis, and the wisest of all wise men. He was a soothsayer of soothsayers. There had been no such master of the craft since or before. If any man lost a reindeer, whom but Urier did he seek?

" He had many reindeer of his own, and had visited many countries. But he grew old, and perceived that all was vanity, and that the world was growing worse and worse. 'The reindeer,' said he, 'fall off in numbers. The moss dies, or ceases to grow. The game decreases. There is nothing but avarice and deceit. I will live no longer in this wicked world, but will go up to heaven !' So he told his two wives to get things ready for a journey, and to harness his reindeer. But he ordered that *everything should be new*,[1] and that no single piece of old stuff was to be either used or packed up. So they got themselves ready for the journey, and harnessed the reindeer to a sledge.

"When all was prepared, he mounted aloft, and drove through the air up into the sky. There were

---

[1] The italics are not in the work quoted.

four male reindeer in each sledge—one sledge for Urier, one for his wives, who followed.

"They had scarcely got half-way when Urier's reindeer fell sick, and could go no further. There was no need to tell him what had been done. He knew it. His second wife had not obeyed his orders, but had put the band of an old jacket in the harness.

"She would rather live on earth with her children, than go to heaven with her husband. So he let her go down. But the other went to heaven with him."[1]

We have been considering both the earliest relations of the Slavonic tribes to Christianity, and their condition before it crossed their path at all. In ending the survey, let us draw a little forward—from the pale shadows of its icy home—the picture of humanity framed in this old Lap legend.

We shall find in it very decided outlines of those passionate yearnings which only the Peace of God can hush. We shall detect in it the very prayer which the tidings of Calvary came to answer.

With all his experience, and his wisdom, and his proficiency in magic, poor Urier, though the master of many reindeer, had discovered the hollowness of the world. Nothing lasted, nothing satisfied, nothing could be confidently relied on. His very strength and faculties were becoming warped by age. "Vanity of vanities! all is vanity," he cried, echoing, though he knew it not, the exclamation of one who, like himself,

---

[1] 'Russian and Turk,' p. 302.

had tasted the most luscious draughts that prosperity could offer. "Behold, all was vanity and vexation of spirit, and there was no profit under the sun."

In the voice of Urier we hear the sighs of heathendom, perplexed by the mysteries of life, and sorrow, and death, and confounded by the discernment of something within every man which nothing without could quiet or appease.

But if earth was unsatisfactory, there was a heaven, where disappointment was unknown. Thither a wise man should obviously betake himself. Thus Urier the Lap issued orders that preparations for departure from this world should be made. But perceiving with a dim uneasiness that, to approach heaven with any hope of admission, a man must be invested with purity unsullied by earth, he declared that *everything used for the journey must be new*. Nevertheless, there was, after all, a flaw in the arrangements. Some lingering relic of the old life below marred the whole, and arrested the upward progress. The earthly element was, however, at last expunged, and fell back into the world which Urier had left behind, after which his ascent was uninterruptedly triumphant.

In the thoughts on which this and similar legends were built, paganism "in the ends of the earth" was blindly stretching out her hands towards an unknown God. "Without holiness no man shall see the Lord:" this was virtually her signal of distress. For Who and where the Lord was, and whence the holiness He demanded was to be derived, she knew not. Old things were to pass away,—so far her instinct taught

her.   But that through the grave and gate of death,—
by the Humility of Bethlehem, the Obedience of
Nazareth, the Anguish of Gethsemane, the Sacrifice
of Calvary,—that thus alone were all things to become new,—this was what she did not know, and
could not guess.   The great problem of life she saw,
but its solution lay beyond her range of vision.

CHAPTER IX.

CONCLUSION.

WE have watched Christianity slowly creeping, like a thread of lambent light, around and among the Slavonic group of nationalities. After many interruptions and many fitful flickerings, the luminous circle is complete. And all that remains is to cast a briefly retrospective glance over the space which we have been traversing.

The remark must be repeated, that the prominent feature in the story now told is the peculiarly persistent opposition encountered by Christian missionaries on Slavonic ground.

To the characteristics and the surroundings and the history of the people, all already dwelt upon at large, this remarkably obstinate antagonism may in a great degree be traced. But this being freely granted, it must also be conceded that no inconsiderable amount of the difficulty which dogged the steps of the missionaries and their supporters was due to their own attitude. They generally failed to see that the always essential qualities of patience and tact were most imperatively needful here. And these graces were consequently in too many instances conspicuous by their absence.

Our grasp of the subject, however, would be very defective, if we omitted to refer the mistakes, the shortcomings, aye, and the crimes which disfigured both those who would convert, and those who would not be converted, to the complexion of the times in which they lived. Allowances based on such a reference must indeed be accorded in every similar case, but their liberality should run parallel, not with a chronological table, but with the particular degree of darkness prevalent in the period under consideration.[1] Pleas which may be urged in extenuation of the barbarism of the earliest ages hold good likewise with respect to the gross ignorance of a much later date.[2] The gloom of the centuries before the Christian era was the gloom also of the Slavs and other heathen nations, who played their part at a stage later, by many hundreds of years, of the world's history.

---

[1] "If we want to understand the religions of antiquity, we must try, as well as we can, to enter into the religious, moral, and political atmosphere of the ancient world. We must become ancients ourselves, otherwise we shall never understand the motives and meaning of their faith."—'Chips from a German Workshop,' vol. i. p. 57.

[2] Note the remark of a great novelist upon the ignorance of some English country districts in the last generation. "Strange lingering echoes of the old demon-worship might perhaps even now be caught by the diligent listener among the grey-haired peasantry; for the rude mind with difficulty associates the ideas of power and benignity. A shadowy conception of power that by much persuasion can be induced to refrain from inflicting harm, is the shape most easily taken by the sense of the Invisible in the minds of men who have always been pressed close by primitive wants."—'Silas Marner,' p. 5.

But it may be objected that the Christian princes and potentates who encouraged, directed, and sometimes personally conducted the missionary enterprises, were in possession of the Light as yet unknown to the pagans, and that their violence, their fury, their contempt for human life, and their indifference to the rights of every human being, were therefore wholly inexcusable.

To this it can only be replied that the action of Christianity has been always very gradual, and usually very slow.

The history of its missions in all parts of the world exemplifies this fact on almost every page. In its progress among nations, it was hindered, and impeded, and compelled over and over again to halt, if not to recede. Similarly, in its contact with individuals, it has won—shall we not say that it still usually wins—its way to empire over the heart of man, not by an impetuous leap, but step by step, here a little and there a little, often checked, often chilled, but never despairingly impatient of ultimate success.

Christian precepts ran counter to all the instincts of such men as the chieftains of Bulgaria and Bohemia, of Poland, and Russia, and Pomerania, in whose veins the wild blood of Scythia was still coursing. The time was not ripe for the imposition of the restraining and tranquillizing hands of Christianity, though her rites were widely administered and accepted. Life was not valued as we value it, and the rights of *personality* were barely perceived, much less worked into the foundations of a creed.

"When we examine the ancient mind all the world over," it has been well said, " one very remarkable want is apparent in it, viz., a true idea of the individuality of man; an adequate conception of him as an independent person, a substantial being in himself, whose life and existence were his own.   Man always figures as an appendage to somebody, the subject to the monarch, the son to the father, the wife to the husband, the slave to the master.   He is the function or circumstance of somebody else.   The slave was a piece of property, κτῆμα ἔμψυχον, and the old Hindu law divided "cattle into bipeds and quadrupeds." The laws of Manu insert the *persons* of the wife and the son *in the person* of the head of the family, as if they were absorbed and incorporated in it, just as the several *members* are absorbed and embraced in the unity of the *body*."   "We see, both in the political institutions and superstitions of antiquity, regulations and practices which obviously imply, as the necessary condition of their existence, a totally different idea of human individuality, and of human rights, from that with which modern society, and Christian society, is animated. — A lawgiver cannot act against the universal opinion of mankind in his day; if he institutes any particular infringement of human rights, there must be a premiss for that infringement in an universal defective conception of mankind at that day.   Thus, the law of Lycurgus for the destruction of weakly infants in Sparta at the very birth, would have been impossible had there not been *all over the world*, then, a very different conception of the right of the human being with respect to his own life, from what exists now. With us, the rights of man commence with his very birth, and an infant an hour old has an independent right and property in his own life which the whole world cannot take away from him. Had that been the received idea in the age of Lycurgus, he could not have founded this Spartan rule; but it was not. Mankind had not embraced, as yet, the true notion of human individuality; man was an appendage to some man or some body. That the infant was treated as the pure property of the State in Sparta, was a result which rose upon an *universal* defective assumption regarding man in *that stage* of human progress; it was a harsh and cruel use of that assumption, but it could not have arisen without that assumption as its condition." — "The same defective idea of human individuality, and the rights of life, is shown in a fact which has a horrible prominence in the history of ancient religions, viz., the prevalence of human sacrifice. It is impossible to suppose that any superstition, however strong, could have so trampled upon the natural right of life, as the custom of human sacrifice did, had there been at the time that idea of the natural right of life existing in the human mind; that is to say, if that idea had existed in any definite shape. The very selfishness of man, and the very instinct of self-preservation, would in that case have made him stand up for his own life, against the claims of a monstrous and cruel power. If we suppose such a strict and accurate sense of the right of the individual to his own life as we have now, no superstition, however ferocious, could possibly have had force enough to withstand that sense, and sacrifice individuals wholesale. There could not, therefore, have been then that strict sense of the right and property of the individual in his own life that there is now ; and the institution of human sacrifice thus implied, as the condition of its own establishment, the defective idea of the rights of the individual man. With these facts before us, we may understand how deeply fixed in the mind of ancient society was the idea of one man belonging to another ; how long a time it must have required to uproot that idea, and how, in truth, nothing but a new religion could do it. Even Rome, with all her later material civilization, could never completely embrace the notion, which lies at the bottom of all modern law and religion, that every man is *himself*, an individual being with an independent existence of his own, and independent rights.   The *jus naturale* of the individual is indeed so self-evident now that we can hardly conceive society without it ; and we are apt to suppose that it must have been equally self-evident to any human being, in any age, who had the simple exercise of his reason. ᐧ But all history shows that, so far from this idea having been always obvious to the human understanding, it has, on the contrary, been the slow and gradual growth of ages.

Nor, perhaps, is the consideration valueless, that in the early stages of society, before civil government was formed, and before man had become a trained and disciplined being, as—in a degree—he is now, some strong idea, such as that contained in saying, "You belong to another, you are the property of another," may have been necessary to control and keep in bounds the native insolence and wild pride, the obstinacy, the fierceness, the animal caprice, the rage, the spite, the passion, of the human creature. When man was rude, and government was weak, there was wanted, for the control of man, some *idea* which could fasten upon him and overcome him, and be in the stead of government and civilization. Such an idea was this one. The nature that can be turned by nothing else can be turned by an idea. Instil from his earliest infancy into man the idea that he *belongs* to another, is the property of another, let everything around proceed upon this idea, let there be nothing to interfere with it, or rouse suspicions in his mind to the contrary, and he will yield entirely to that idea. He will take his own deprivation of right, the necessity of his own subservience to another, as a matter of course. And that idea of himself will keep him in order. He will grow up with the impression that he has not the right of ownership in himself, in his passions, any more than he has in his work. He will thus be coerced from *within himself*, but not *by* himself; *i.e.*, not by an active faculty of self-command, but by the passive reception of an instilled notion which he has admitted into his own mind, and which has fastened upon him so strongly that he cannot shake it off."[1]

[1] Prof. Mozley's 'Ruling Ideas in Early Ages,' pp. 38, 39, and 41, 42, 43.

No apology is needed for the transcription of these passages at length, since it would be impossible to express in more forcible or appropriate words, the considerations which must be duly marshalled and weighed if we would arrive at a correct estimate of the people, to the record of whose words and ways this little volume has been devoted.

The period and its people must be balanced together, for the first ruled the possibilities of the second. Here and there, in almost every age, it is true, the attention is caught by some exceptional character, the *avant courier* of a progressive enlightenment, the standard-bearer whose ensign is foreign to the eyes of his fellow-men. But the main body of humanity can only be expected to be abreast, and not ahead, of their day.

That the *outward* profession of Christianity is compatible with conduct of a most defective, not to say contradictory, description, our daily observation amply testifies. But even when the change is inward and real, it is not announced to us by the sudden and brilliant effects of a transformation-scene. Into howsoever "good" ground the seed has fallen, it is for the most part silently, by slow degrees, and under manifold difficulties, that the hundred-fold, or the sixty-fold, or even the thirty-fold, is brought forth. If the biographies of saints of every type are to be allowed as evidence, it is plain that the spiritual life, despite its secret joys, expands with tears, and toils, and struggles.

Thus reflecting, we shall perhaps cease to marvel

that the characters of the turbulent princes and
excitable priests, whose swords gleamed above
the baptismal waters as an alternative too well
understood by the unbaptized, were not trans-
figured in their own passage from paganism to
Christianity.

That more might have been done, and that what
was accomplished would have been more durable, had
a holy life, instead of a drawn sword, been the method
of appeal, cannot well be doubted. Proofs of this,
indeed, are furnished in the occasional exceptions to
the rule of coercion which relieve the picture.

It must not, however, be forgotten, that apart
from the imperfect civilization and the slender
knowledge of the period, another source of the
fierceness which we deprecate in the Slavonic missioners, is to be found in the then prevalent influence
of the Crusades.

Into the current of this mighty movement, together
with much that was truly noble and self-renouncing,
every species of fanaticism, violence, and impetuosity
had flung itself.

The passionate impulse spread and deepened until
it inflamed alike soldiers and monks, citizens and
ecclesiastics, princes and peasants.

In the heterogeneous medley of devotees the tares
and the wheat were indiscriminately confused. Motives
were mingled, objects obscured, judgment distorted,
personal vehemence unchained,—and as this vast
complex influence swept like a torrent across Christendom, it infected, inevitably, every spring of mis-

sionary effort.[1]   Against its impetus, such milder modes of conversion as were moulded upon Apostolic models could not preserve their equilibrium.

The *attractive* power of the Cross thus disclosed itself rather in spite of the system which enforced external Christianity, than on the strength of it.   How singular, as they unfolded themselves by degrees before pagan eyes, the Christian doctrines must have at first appeared to heathendom, is instructively brought home to us in the subjoined words of a writer already laid under contribution in the earlier pages of this book.

"Let us begin with that which we found to be characteristic of the Asiatic mind,—the reverence for physical strength.

"Nothing can be more clear on the very surface of the Gospel narrative than that the standard of heroism there contemplated is precisely of the opposite nature.

"The individuality of the Brahmin has sunk into nothingness before his admiration of that active power which he beheld in the world of nature; the individuality of the Christian rose into moral significance in the presence of a contrary thought, the belief that the highest strength was that passive power which could sustain physical weakness.

[1] "Much as they—the Crusades—subserved the interest of the papacy, entangled the relations of the Greek and Latin Church, united nations and parts of nations by one great idea, and modified in many ways the general spirit of the times, they wrought no lasting changes in the area of the Christian fold."
—Hardwick's 'Middle Age,' p. 236.

" The object which the Christian idealized was not so much a life that could do great things, as a life that could bear great things ; not so much a power to work, as a power to suffer ; not so much a strength that shone forth in outward majesty, as a strength that manifested itself in supporting outward meanness.

" This is, indeed, the distinctive and characteristic element in the Christian ideal ; it permeates the whole narrative like an atmosphere. The eye, in the fourth Gospel, is summoned to rest upon One Who, voluntarily and deliberately, exchanges a Divine for a human form,—refuses to grasp the empire of Godhead, in order that He may wear the garb of a servant, divests Himself of an element of Life which is natural to Him, in order that He may incorporate an element of death which is foreign to His nature, —empties His omniscience into a human knowledge, His infinitude into a finite form, His eternity into a temporal duration, His power of universal dominion into a power of absolute service.

" The narrative is constructed in such a way, that in proportion as the human limitations cluster around the Life of the Master, the reader is made more and more conscious of the Master's essential majesty, sees His strength just where He is physically most weak, and beholds His spiritual triumph precisely on that field where He is physically vanquished,—the Death of the Cross."

Further. The worship of His disciples is that of "a strength which is strong by becoming weak ;" their reverence, that of " a Life which is individually great by losing its own individuality, and living in the lives of others. They find heroism precisely in those qualities whose opposites had been the worship of the Asiatic intellect. They assign a kingdom to poverty of spirit, an increase of knowledge to the increase of sorrow, an earthly empire to the power of gentleness, a perfect satisfaction to the hungering and thirsting of the soul. They see a higher triumph in the peace-maker than in the war-maker, a superior strength in the power of forgiveness to that which dwells in the capacity for vengeance. They find the most promising subjects of the new kingdom precisely in those whom the Asiatic intellect would have passed over,—in the labouring, the heavy-laden, the con-sciously weak, and poor, and needy."

Once more. "The common assent of Christen-dom" had been indicated by St. Paul "to a new association of the beautiful,—an association which, to the heathen mind, appeared the wildest of paradoxes, —the union of glory and pain. Christ was Himself the personification of the new æsthetic ideal. He unites in one act the hitherto opposite elements of glory and of shame. He looks forward to the hour of deepest human frailty, as the hour in which the Son of Man should be glorified. He declares on the road to Emmaus, that the disharmony was an essen-tial part of the beauty, that Christ must needs have suffered, that He might enter into His glory. He stands under the shadow of the Cross, and bequeaths to the world His Peace,—He confronts the spectacle of death, and speaks of the fulness of His Joy."—

" He proposed to conquer the heart of the world, and to conquer it by the exhibition of His own Heart. The founders of previous kingdoms had sought to rule by placing in the foreground the display of their personal superiority : the Founder of Christianity resolved to subjugate mankind by the sacrifice of Himself. The kings of former time had fought their way to empire by shedding the blood of their enemies ; the Aspirant to this new kingdom determined to secure dominion by shedding His own." [1]

The foregoing reflections possess a double value for us as we review the history of the evangelization of the Slavs. For, first, they collect, and present in a sharp and concise antithesis, the numerous points on which the heathen and the Christian ideals clashed.

And secondly, they throw into strong relief the winning combination of those very characteristics of our Blessed Redeemer, which could not but appeal to the feelings of such early Slavonians as were confronted with the Divine Portrait. The participation of their race in the power and grandeur of this world was, in most instances, very small. They had long been schooled, on the contrary, in the endurance for which we noticed them at the outset to be naturally qualified.[2]

[1] ' The Originality of the Character of Christ.'—*Contemporary Review*, November, 1878.

[2] Cf. ' Silas Marner,' p. 5, again. " To them pain and mishap present a far wider range of possibilities than gladness or enjoyment : their imagination is almost barren of the images that feed desire and hope, but is all overgrown by recollections

But in those cases—unhappily too few—where the Divine Picture was suffered to plead Its own cause, where a Voice, crying in the wilderness, bespoke attention, instead of a sword flashing to command submission,—what an effect must again and again have been produced !

For here was another and a glorious side to the lot which these men had learnt to bear in sullen, stolid apathy.

Here was One Who had spontaneously incurred the very conditions which rendered their own lives well-nigh unendurable. And further—if, indeed, the Story was not too sweet to be quite true—it was for their sakes that He had stooped so low ! If this was the Shepherd who came to seek and to save those who were lost, what a home must His fold be for the weary and the heavy-laden !

But we have marked that, save in the ministrations of bishop Otho of Bamberg, and of such as he, the "green pastures and the still waters" were not put prominently forward among the inducements to a change of creed. They could be known, we must never forget, to but few among the propagandists themselves.

In the dying words of Vladimir Monomachus,[1]

that are a perpetual pasture to fear." Spoken of illiterate English peasants in their old age, these words are not less pointedly applicable to the people of Slavonic birth and experience, whose characters it has been our endeavour to analyse. The Pomeranians, it will be remembered, displayed a quite exceptional gaiety of demeanour.—P. 109.

[1] Or, 'The second,' A.D. 1113.

addressed to his sons, an echo remains to us of the genuine, practical piety occasionally to be found among the rough princes of the dimly-lighted ages into which we have been peering. A few sentences may here be given.

"O, my children," said this Russian Christian, conscious that his life was drawing rapidly to an end, "praise God, and love man. For it is not fasting, nor solitude, nor monastic life, that will procure you eternal life, but only doing good. Forget not the poor, nourish them; remember that riches come from God, and are given you only for a short time. Do not bury your wealth in the ground; this is against the precepts of Christianity. Be fathers to orphans. Be judges in the cause of widows, and do not let the powerful oppress the weak. Put to death neither innocent nor guilty, for nothing is so sacred as the life and the soul of a Christian. Never take the Name of God in vain, and never break the oath you have made in kissing the crucifix."

"My brethren said to me, 'Help us to drive out the sons of Rostislav, or else give up our alliance.' But I said, I cannot forget that I have kissed the cross. I opened then the Book of Psalms, and read there with deep emotion, 'Why art thou so vexed, O my soul? and why art thou so disquieted within me? Put thy trust in God. I will confess my faults, and He is gracious.'

"Be not envious at the triumph of the wicked, and the success of treachery. Fear the lot of the impious. Do not desert the sick; do not let the sight of dead corpses terrify you, for we must all die. Receive with joy the blessing of the clergy; do not keep yourselves aloof from them; do them good, that they may pray to God for you. Drive out of your heart all suggestions of pride, and remember that we are all perishable—to-day full of hope, to-morrow in the coffin. Abhor lying, drunkenness, and debauchery. Love your wives, but do not suffer them to have any power over you. Endeavour constantly to obtain knowledge. Without having quitted his palace, my father spoke five languages; a thing which wins for us the admiration of foreigners."[1]

The discourse then goes on to exhort to prudence and vigilance in war, recommending ejaculatory prayer when on horseback, should fuller devotions be impracticable. Princely mercy and hospitality are earnestly inculcated, and the duties of activity and diligence strongly urged upon the attention of the hearers.

The devotional aspirations of the dying king are quaintly intermingled with complacent memories of his exploits in war and in the chase. He recapitulates instances of his industry, his charity, his conquests, his intrepidity, his justice, and dwells with especial satisfaction on his capabilities as a traveller. "No one," says he, "has ever travelled more rapidly than I have done! Setting out in the morning from Tchernigof, I have arrived at Kief before the hour of vespers." But beneath the whole of this curious

[1] Stanley's 'Eastern Church,' p. 313.

monologue there runs an under-current of thankful recognition of the Hand Which had upheld him in so many adventures, and delivered him from so many and great dangers. "Oh! my children," he exclaims,—and these are his last words, as he lay in full view of that shadowy "under world," which to his ancestors was a mere outlet from the domain of visible phenomena, as fearful as it was vague,—"Oh! my children! fear neither death nor wild beasts. Trust in Providence; it far surpasses all human precautions."[1]

The Russian primate had commended to the attention of this Vladimir Monomachus—probably on his accession to the throne—the 101st Psalm, as a suitable framework for a monarch's meditation, as well as a model on which he might with advantage shape his life and his administration.

The king committed it to memory.

Let its injunctions, which a prince of the type and times of Vladimir II. believed himself able to carry out from beginning to end, close our examination of the Conversion of the Slavs.

I. *I will sing of mercy and judgment: unto Thee, O Lord, will I sing.*

II. *I will behave myself wisely in a perfect way. O when wilt Thou come unto me? I will walk within my house with a perfect heart.*

III. *I will set no wicked thing before mine eyes: I hate the work of them that turn aside; it shall not cleave to me.*

---

[1] Karamsin, ii. 202, quoted in Stanley's 'Eastern Church,' p. 314.

IV. *A froward heart shall depart from me: I will not know a wicked person.*

V. *Whoso privily slandereth his neighbour, him will I cut off: him that hath an high look and a proud heart will not I suffer.*

VI. *Mine eyes shall be upon the faithful in the land, that they may dwell with me: he that walketh in a perfect way, he shall serve me.*

VII. *He that worketh deceit shall not dwell within my house: he that telleth lies shall not tarry in my sight.*

VIII. *I will early destroy all the wicked of the land; that I may cut off all wicked doers from the city of the Lord.*

THE END.

WYMAN AND SONS, PRINTERS, GREAT QUEEN STREET, LONDON.

Society for Promoting Christian Knowledge.

NON-CHRISTIAN RELIGIOUS SYSTEMS.

Fcap. 8vo., Cloth boards, price 2s. 6d. each, with Map.

BUDDHISM:
Being a Sketch of the Life and Teachings of Gautama, the Buddha. By T. W. RHYS DAVIDS, of the Middle Temple.

HINDUISM.
By MONIER WILLIAMS, M.A., D.C.L., &c.

ISLAM AND ITS FOUNDER.
By J. W. H. STOBART, B.A., Principal, La Martinière College, Lucknow.

THE HEATHEN WORLD AND ST. PAUL.

Fcap. 8vo., Cloth boards, price 2s. each, with Map.

ST. PAUL IN DAMASCUS AND ARABIA.
By the Rev. GEORGE RAWLINSON, M.A., Canon of Canterbury, Camden Professor of Ancient History, Oxford.

ST. PAUL IN GREECE.
By the Rev. G. S. DAVIES, M.A., Charterhouse, Godalming.

ST. PAUL AT ROME.
By the Very Rev. CHARLES MERIVALE, D.D., D.C.L., Dean of Ely.

ST. PAUL IN ASIA MINOR, AND AT THE SYRIAN ANTIOCH.
By the Rev. E. H. PLUMPTRE, D.D., Prebendary of St. Paul's, Vicar of Bickley, Kent, and Professor of New Testament Exegesis in King's College, London.

RECENT PUBLICATIONS.

s. d.

LESSER LIGHTS; or, Some of the Minor
Characters of Scripture traced, with a View to Instruction and
Example in Daily Life. By the Rev. F. BOURDILLON, M.A.,
Author of " Bedside Readings," &c. Post 8vo. ... *Cloth Boards* 2 6

NATURAL HISTORY OF THE BIBLE, THE : being
a Review of the Physical Geography, Geology, and Meteorology
of the Holy Land, with a description of every Animal and
Plant mentioned in Holy Scripture. By the Rev. Canon
TRISTRAM. Third Edition. Crown 8vo. With numerous
Illustrations..*Cloth Boards* 7 6

NARRATIVE OF A MODERN PILGRIMAGE
THROUGH PALESTINE ON HORSEBACK, AND WITH TENTS. By
the Rev. ALFRED CHARLES SMITH, M.A., Christ Church,
Oxford; Rector of Yatesbury, Wilts, Author of " The
Attractions of the Nile," &c. &c. Crown 8vo. With numerous
Illustrations and Four Coloured Plates .... *Cloth Boards* 5 0

SCENES IN THE EAST. — Containing Twelve
Coloured Photographic Views of Places mentioned in the Bible.
By the Rev. Canon TRISTRAM, Author of "The Land of
Israel," &c. 4to. ....*Cloth Boards* 7 6

SCRIPTURE MANNERS AND CUSTOMS : being an
Account of the Domestic Habits, Arts, &c., of Eastern Nations,
mentioned in Holy Scripture. Sixteenth Edition. Fcap. 8vo.
With numerous Wood-cuts . ...*Cloth Boards* 4 0

SINAI AND JERUSALEM ; or, Scenes from Bible
Lands, consisting of Coloured Photographic Views of Places
mentioned in the Bible, including a Panoramic View of
Jerusalem. With Descriptive Letterpress by the Rev. F. W.
HOLLAND, M.A., Honorary Secretary to the Palestine
Exploration Fund .... *Cloth, Bevelled Boards, gilt edges* 7 6

ST. PAUL : THE CITIES VISITED BY. By the
Rev. Professor STANLEY LEATHES, M.A., King's College,
London. Fcap. 8vo. With Nine Wood-cuts ....*Limp cloth* 1 0

TURNING POINTS OF ENGLISH CHURCH
HISTORY. By the Rev. EDWARD L. CUTTS, B.A., Author
of " Some Chief Truths of Religion," " St. Cedd's Cross," &c.
Crown 8vo. ....*Cloth Boards* 3 6

TURNING POINTS OF GENERAL CHURCH
HISTORY. By the Rev. E. L. CUTTS, B.A., Author of
"Pastoral Counsels," &c. Crown 8vo. ....*Cloth Boards* 5 0

Society for Promoting Christian Knowledge.

ANCIENT HISTORY FROM THE MONUMENTS.

Fcap. 8vo., Cloth boards, price 2s. each, with Illustrations.

ASSYRIA, FROM THE EARLIEST TIMES TO THE FALL OF NINEVEH.

By the late GEORGE SMITH, Esq., of the Department of Oriental Antiquities, British Museum.

BABYLONIA, THE HISTORY OF.

By the late GEORGE SMITH, Esq. Edited by the Rev. A. H. SAYCE, Assistant Professor of Comparative Philology, Oxford.

EGYPT, FROM THE EARLIEST TIMES TO B.C. 300.

By S. BIRCH, LL.D., &c.

GREEK CITIES AND ISLANDS OF ASIA MINOR.

By W. S. W. VAUX, M.A., F.R.S.

PERSIA, FROM THE EARLIEST PERIOD TO THE ARAB CONQUEST.

By W. S. W. VAUX, M.A., F.R.S.

Also in Preparation.

SINAI, FROM THE FOURTH EGYPTIAN DYNASTY TO THE PRESENT DAY.

By H. S. PALMER, Major, Royal Engineers, F.R.A.S.

DEPOSITORIES :

77, GREAT QUEEN STREET, LINCOLN'S-INN FIELDS, W.C. ;
4, ROYAL EXCHANGE, E.C. ; AND 48, PICCADILLY, W. ;
LONDON.

www.ingramcontent.com/pod-product-compliance
Lightning Source LLC
Chambersburg PA
CBHW020627030726
47497CB00007B/2449